"I won't marry Lorenzo now."

"Certainly not," Lorenzo's mother replied. "But I have another son. I agree he's done little to recommend himself to you, but Renato is to blame for this and Renato must put it right." Baptista continued in her most regal manner, "Your marriage should take place immediately."

There was one moment's total, thunderstruck silence. Heather tried to speak, but couldn't.

"In my day a young woman knew better than to laugh at an eligible match," Baptista said with haughty disapproval.

"But Renato isn't an eligible match," Heather pointed out. "One, he doesn't want to marry *anyone*. Two, he doesn't want to marry *me*. Three, hell will freeze over before I marry him. It's out of the question."

"You came here to marry a son of this house, and that's what you must do."

Dear Reader,

Being married to an Italian, I take a special delight in writing about Italian men—the most fascinating and endearing men on earth. I've enjoyed telling the stories of the three Martelli brothers.

Although linked by kinship, they are all different. Lorenzo, the youngest, is a merry charmer. Bernardo is aloof, a loner. Renato, the eldest, is head of the family, a man of confidence and power. But his power is a two-edged sword, and his reliance on it nearly destroys his life and that of Heather, the woman who loves him.

And then there is Sicily, their home, one of the most beautiful places on earth, where people's true passions rise to the surface, giving them the courage to follow their hearts.

Wife by Arrangement is about Heather and Renato, the story of how a woman disarms a strong man by teaching just how powerful love can be. Look out next month for *Husband by Necessity*.

With best wishes,

Lucy Gordon

WIFE BY ARRANGEMENT
Lucy Gordon

The Italian Grooms

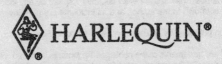

HARLEQUIN®

TORONTO • NEW YORK • LONDON
AMSTERDAM • PARIS • SYDNEY • HAMBURG
STOCKHOLM • ATHENS • TOKYO • MILAN • MADRID
PRAGUE • WARSAW • BUDAPEST • AUCKLAND

This book is for Nikki Little
who gave generously of her time.

ISBN 0-373-03655-8

WIFE BY ARRANGEMENT

First North American Publication 2001.

Copyright © 2001 by Lucy Gordon.

Visit us at www.eHarlequin.com

Printed in U.S.A.

CHAPTER ONE

'HEY, Heather—your Sicilian lover is here.'

Heather looked up self-consciously. 'Lorenzo isn't my lover!' she insisted. 'Just—just—'

'Just good friends?' Sally suggested wickedly. 'Well, if the man out there isn't your lover, he ought to be. Big and sexy with ''come to bed'' eyes. If he was mine, I wouldn't waste time *not* sleeping with him.'

'Will you keep your voice down?' Heather said frantically, aware that every woman in the staff room was regarding her with interest. She was taking her afternoon break from the perfume counter of Gossways, London's most luxurious department store. The worldly-wise Sally was on the next counter.

Heather got to her feet, smiling at the thought of Lorenzo Martelli, the light-hearted, handsome young man who had swept into her life a month ago and made her head spin.

'I didn't know you knew Lorenzo by sight,' she told Sally.

'I don't, but he asked for you. Besides, he looks just like a Sicilian should: incredibly sensual, as if he'd take a woman to bed as soon as look at her. Hurry up and get out there, or I'll have him myself!'

Heather chuckled and returned to her counter, eager to see Lorenzo. He'd come to England on a business trip that was supposed to last two weeks, but he'd been enchanted by Heather's quiet charm and stayed on, unable to tear himself away from her. They were going out together tonight. Now she was delighted at the thought of seeing him early.

But it wasn't Lorenzo.

Lorenzo was tall, fair, curly-haired, in his late twenties. This man was past thirty. There was a slight scar on one side of his face and his features, which were too irregular to be handsome, were marred by a touch of harshness.

He was tall and heavily built, his shoulders wide, his hair black. He had the dark eyes and olive skin of the southern Italian, but he had something more. Heather couldn't put a name to it, but she knew at once why Sally, who judged each man by his bedworthiness, had reacted strongly. It was because he judged every woman the same way. It was there in his eyes, that were lazy without ever quite being off guard: the instinctive question—do I want to sleep with her? Yes? No? Probably yes. How much of a challenge would she be?

Heather was startled to receive such a look. Her fine features were pretty without being beautiful. Her hair was very light brown, but not exactly blonde, and although her slim figure was graceful it wasn't voluptuous. At twenty-three she'd never known the tribute of a wolf whistle, and no man had ever raked her up and down as this one was doing.

'Are you the gentleman who was asking for me?' she asked.

He glanced at the nameplate pinned to her white blouse. 'I am.'

His voice was dark and deep, with an accent that coloured the words without obscuring them. Not like Lorenzo's light, teasing tones.

'You were recommended by a friend of mine whom you served—a Mr Charles Smith, but you won't remember him among so many customers. I'm buying for several ladies, including my mother. She's in her sixties, very respectable, but perhaps secretly wishing her life had been a little more exciting.'

'I know what she'd like,' Heather said, producing a fragrance that was a little daring, but not outrageous. She was touched and impressed by this man's understanding of his mother.

'That will suit her perfectly,' he said. 'But now we come to the more delicate part of the business. I have a lady-friend—beautiful, sensual, with very expensive tastes. Her name is Elena, and her personality is extravagant, mysterious and passionate.' His eyes met hers. 'I'm sure you understand.'

In a flash she found herself understanding all sorts of things. For instance, how Elena would be very drawn to this man who, despite his lack of conventional beauty, had an impressiveness that—she put a firm brake on her thoughts.

'Perfectly, sir,' she said crisply. 'I'd suggest "Deep of the Night".'

'It sounds just like her,' he agreed shamelessly.

She rubbed a drop of the perfume on her wrist and held it out to him. He inhaled slowly, then took her wrist between his fingers and brought it close to his face. She had a sudden impression of fierce, controlled power behind his civilised manner, as though she'd been strolling through a sedate garden and seen a tiger lurking behind the leaves, ready to spring. She resisted the impulse to snatch her hand back.

'Admirable,' he said. 'I'll take the large flagon.'

Heather almost gasped. The large flagon was the costliest item in a very costly range. Her commission on this sale was beginning to look very good. Perhaps even good enough to buy a really beautiful wedding dress...

She stopped that thought in its tracks. It was undignified to hope for something that probably wouldn't happen.

'Now, another lady, with a different personality—light-hearted and fun.'

'"Summer Dance" might suit her. It's fresh and flowery—'

'But not naive?' he asked anxiously.

'Certainly not. Insouciant but sophisticated.'

She tested it on the other arm and again he took her wrist, holding it a quarter-inch from his face. Heather could feel his warm breath against her skin and she wished he would let her go. But that was an absurd over-reaction, she told herself sensibly. He wasn't looking at her. His eyes were closed and he was in a faraway world, with his various mistresses. His hold on her wrist was quite impersonal.

But then the thought crept in that nothing was impersonal with him. This was a man with whom everything— every kind word, every cruel one, every insult, every wound to his pride, every gesture of love—would be taken deeply personally. And for that reason he was very, very dangerous: perhaps the most dangerous man she had ever encountered. When he opened his eyes and looked at her she realised that she'd been holding her breath.

'Perfetto,' he murmured. 'How well we understand each other.'

He released her and she felt as though she were awakening from a dream. She could still feel the pressure on her wrist where he'd held it with such soft, yet irresistible power. She pulled herself firmly together.

'I try to understand all my customers, signore,' she replied. 'It's my job.'

He made a face of appreciation. 'Signore? So you understand Italian?'

She smiled. 'I know some Italian and about ten words of Sicilian.'

She didn't know what had made her mention Sicilian, except perhaps a desire to know if this man really did come from the same part of the world as Lorenzo. It seemed that he did.

He regarded her with amused curiosity, murmuring, 'I wonder why you are learning my dialect.'

'I'm not exactly learning it,' she disclaimed hastily. 'I just picked up a few words from a friend.'

'And doubtless your friend is a handsome young man. Has he yet told you that you are *grazziusu*?'

'I think we should concentrate on your purchases,' Heather said, hoping she wasn't blushing. Lorenzo had used exactly that word to her only the night before, explaining that it was one of the many Sicilian words for beautiful. She shouldn't be talking like this with a stranger. But he was like a magician, who could twist the conversation this way and that with a wave of an invisible wand. He had said *grazziusu* with a soft, seductive power that even Lorenzo, in his ardour, hadn't matched.

'I see that you understand the word, and not from a dictionary,' he observed. 'I'm glad your lover appreciates you.'

No wonder this man had several mistresses if he went about talking like this. Doubtless she too was supposed to be flattered. But she refused to go weak at the knees. It had been a long day, and her legs were tired. That was all.

'Shall we return to the matter in hand?' she asked.

'If we must. What next?'

Heather regarded him levelly. 'Let me get this clear, *signore*. Just how many lady-friends are you trying to—er—keep happy?'

He grinned shamelessly, giving an eloquent shrug. 'Is it important?'

'It is if they have different personalities.'

'Very different,' he confirmed. 'I like one to suit each mood. Minetta is light-hearted, Julia is musical, and Elena is darkly sensual.'

He was trying to unsettle her; there was no doubt of it. His eyes spoke meanings that went far beyond what his lips were saying. She observed briskly, 'Well, that should make things nice and simple.'

'Simple?'

'A man of only three moods.'

She was startled at herself. A good sales assistant thought only of the sale. She didn't backchat the customer and risk offending him. But he wasn't offended. He even seemed amused at her swift riposte.

'You're quite right,' he said. 'Three isn't enough. I have a vacancy for a witty lady, which you could fill perfectly.'

'Oh, I wouldn't suit you at all,' she fenced.

'I'm not so sure about that.'

'*I* am. Completely sure.'

'I wonder why.' He was laughing.

Heather laughed back. She was beginning to take his measure. 'Well, for a start, I'd never agree to be part of a crowd. You'd have to get rid of all the others.'

'I'm sure you'd make it worth my while.'

'If I felt that *you* were worth it,' she said daringly. 'But you wouldn't be, because I'm not in the market.'

'Ah, yes, of course! You already have a lover.'

There was that word again. Why was the whole world harping on lovers all of a sudden?

'Let's just say that I have a young man who suits me.'

'And he comes from Sicily, since you are learning his

language. Which also means that you're hoping to marry him.'

To her dismay Heather felt a revealing blush creep over her face. To cover it she spoke sharply. 'If you mean that I've set my cap at him, you're wrong. And this conversation is over.'

'Forgive me. It's not my business.'

'Indeed it isn't.'

'But I hope he isn't leading you on a fool's dance, seducing you with hints of marriage, and then vanishing back to his own country.'

'I'm not that easily seduced. Neither by him nor—by anyone,' she finished hastily, wondering why her mind had scurried down that particular by-path.

'Then you haven't allowed him into your bed. That's either very neglectful of him, or very clever of you. I wonder which.'

Indignantly she challenged him with a direct gaze, and what she saw startled her. Despite the teasing sensuality of his words, his eyes held the same dispassionate calculation he would have shown to a high-priced purchase.

'You don't dress like the others,' he remarked. 'Why?'

It was true. Heather was perfectly made-up and her long hair was elegantly styled, courtesy of the store's beauty parlour. But whereas the other assistants, with their employer's encouragement, dressed in slightly provocative styles, Heather stuck firmly to conventional clothes. Her skirt was black, her blouse was snow-white and fresh. Her boss had suggested that she might 'put herself about more', but she had refused, and since her sales figures were excellent the matter had been allowed to drop.

'I think,' the man persisted, 'it's because you're a proud and subtle woman—too proud to put everything in the window. And subtle enough to know that when a woman holds back she's at her most alluring. By covering yourself up you make a man wonder how you would look without clothes.'

It was a direct, frontal attack from a man with all the nerve in the world, and something in Heather was wryly appreciative even while something else warned her to put him firmly in his place.

'Can I interest you in anything more, sir?' she asked primly.

'You could interest me in a good deal,' he responded at once. 'Let me take you to dinner, and we can discuss my interest in you.'

'That wasn't what I—still, I suppose I could have phrased that question more cleverly, couldn't I?'

'I thought you phrased it perfectly. I'm interested; I've made that plain. And I'm a generous man. I doubt your boyfriend will marry you. He'll disappear, leaving you with a broken heart.'

'And you'll leave me dancing for joy, I suppose?' she couldn't resist answering.

'It depends what makes you dance for joy. Shall we say ten thousand pounds to start with? Play your cards right, and I think you could do very well out of me.'

'And I think the sooner you leave you the better. I'm not interested in you or your money, and if you say another word I shall call Security.'

'Twenty thousand pounds.'

'Shall I gift-wrap these items for you, sir, or have you changed your mind now you know you'll get nothing from me?'

'What do you think?'

'I think you'd better find a woman who's selling herself. I'm only selling perfume. I take it you don't want these.'

He shrugged. 'There'd hardly be any point, would there? Of course, it's a shame about the commission you would have earned.'

'Commission be blowed!' Heather said very deliberately. 'The store is about to close. Goodbye! Don't come back!'

He gave her a grin that contained a hint of challenge, and walked out with the air of a man who'd achieved something, although for the life of her she couldn't think what.

She was furious, both with him and herself. He'd raised false hopes for her pay packet, and he'd insulted her. But, far worse, for a brief moment he'd persuaded her to find him charming. Part of her had enjoyed the light-hearted game she'd thought they were playing. But then she'd seen the cold calculation in his eyes, and she'd known that the woman who went to this man's bed for money would be a fool. And the woman who did it for love would be an even greater fool.

She hurried home. Her flatmate was out so she had the place to herself as she prepared for the evening ahead with Lorenzo Martelli, the young man Sally called 'her lover'. He wasn't her lover, nor had he tried to urge her into bed, for which she liked him more.

In the month she'd known him she seemed to have been under a spell, something lovelier than reality, with none of reality's pain and trouble. She didn't call it love, because the word 'love' summoned up Peter, and a wilderness of suffering at the brutal way he'd dumped her. She only knew that Lorenzo had charmed her out of her sadness.

She'd met him through a buyer in the Gossways Food Hall. The Martellis dealt in Sicilian fruit and vegetables, much of which they grew on the vast family estates around Palermo. What they couldn't supply themselves they bought in from other growers, taking nothing but the very best. Even so, Gossways had a special deal under which it accepted only produce grown by the Martellis themselves. Lorenzo had recently been appointed export manager of the business, and was visiting customers, introducing himself.

He lived like a young king at the Ritz Hotel. Sometimes he took her to eat there; sometimes they found a tiny place by the river. But always there was a gift, sometimes valuable, sometimes silly, given with a tribute in his eyes. She didn't know what it might mean for the future. Lorenzo had a touch of the playboy whose charm and looks won his way through life. She guessed that back in Sicily there were a dozen young women who would be disappointed if he were to marry. Of course, she wasn't counting on marriage. She told herself that many times. She knew that his charm and admiration were doing her a world of good, and when he left without her she would cope somehow.

Tonight she found his message on the answer-machine, urging her to wear the pale blue silk dress he'd bought for her, which brought out the dark blue of her eyes. They were large eyes, and they gave her face distinction, even beauty.

As always he arrived five minutes before the agreed time, with a red rose, which he gave her with a flourish, and a pearl necklace which he'd bought to go with the dress.

The sight of him made her smile with happiness. He was a handsome young giant, six foot two, with a booming laugh and good-natured grin that invited the whole world to share his pleasure.

'Tonight is a great occasion,' he told her. 'My older brother, Renato, has arrived from Sicily.' He added ruefully, 'I should have gone home two weeks ago. He knows I stayed because of you, and now he wants to meet you. We are his guests at the Ritz tonight.'

'But we were going to the theatre—'

'Could you bear not to? I have rather neglected business recently—' he flicked her cheek gently '—all your fault.'

'Tossing me into the lions' den, huh?' she asked with a chuckle.

He put his arm around her. 'We'll go in together.'

On the short journey to the Ritz he talked about his brother, who ran the vast family estates in Sicily. By hard work and shrewd dealing he'd transformed the vineyards and olive groves, making them produce three times as much, buying up land, expanding, making Martelli the top name in fine produce in every luxury store and hotel throughout the world.

'He thinks of nothing but work,' Lorenzo complained. 'How he can make more money, and more money. Me, I prefer spending it.'

'I'm sure he knows that. He wants to see who you're spending it on.' She touched the pearls, which were elegant and restrained, but clearly expensive.

'He's ready to like you. Trust me.' As they reached the Ritz and he handed her from the taxi, Lorenzo murmured, 'Don't be afraid of him.'

'I'm not. Are *you* afraid of him?'

'No way. But he's the head of the family, and in Sicily that's very important. However fierce he was, he was always my wonderful big brother who'd stick by me, help sort out my problems—'

'Deal with the girls' fathers?' Heather suggested mischievously.

Lorenzo cleared his throat. 'That's all in the past. Let's go in.'

Heather was curious to meet this man who was so important in Lorenzo's life. She looked around at the luxurious restaurant with its elegant marble and floor-to-ceiling French windows, hung with heavy red curtains.

On the far side a man sat alone at a table. He rose as they approached him, a polite smile of welcome on his face. Heather strove to match it through the tide of indignation that welled up in her.

'Good evening, *signorina*,' Renato Martelli said, giving her a courteous little bow. 'It is a pleasure to meet you.'

'You mean, meet me *again*, don't you?' she asked coolly. 'You surely can't have forgotten our encounter in Gossways this afternoon?'

'What's this?' Lorenzo asked. 'You've met before?'

'Earlier today,' Renato Martelli confirmed. 'I was impatient to see the lady of whom I've heard so much, so I adopted a subterfuge, for which I hope I'll be forgiven.' He was smiling as he raised her hand to his lips.

Heather regarded him wryly. 'I'll think about it,' she said.

Renato gallantly pulled out a gilt-and-plush chair for her, and the three of them sat down.

'What subterfuge?' Lorenzo asked, looking from one to the other.

'Your brother came to my counter, posing as a customer,' Heather told him.

'I thought we could assess each other in a more natural atmosphere,' Renato explained.

'Each other?' she murmured.

'I'm sure you formed your own opinion of me.'

'Oh, yes,' she assured him. 'I certainly did.'

She left it there. She was far from finished but she didn't want to look as though she were sulking. A waiter appeared with the menu and when he'd given the order Renato added, 'And a bottle of your very finest champagne.'

At this hint of approval Lorenzo grinned. Perversely Heather found herself even more annoyed. Was she supposed to jump for joy because Renato Martelli had tossed her a crumb of favour?

She would never have guessed they were brothers. She knew that over the centuries the island of Sicily had been invaded so often that many racial types—Greek, Arab, Italian, French, Spanish, Celtic—were mixed in its inhabitants. There was something Greek in Lorenzo's fine looks, blue eyes and light brown curly hair. Despite his size his movements were graceful.

She guessed Renato was one of those men who had come to manhood in his early teens. It was hard to picture him as a boy. Perhaps an Italian ancestor had given him those vivid looks, but the air of haughty pride came from a Spaniard, and there was something Celtic in the mobility of his face, the sensuality of his wide mouth.

His features were fierce and irregular, and at first sight he was put in the shade by his beautiful younger brother. But there was a dark glitter in his eyes that compelled attention, and he had an extra something that made looks irrelevant. In a room full of handsome men, Renato Martelli would be the one women looked at, and wondered about.

He was powerfully built, with a massiveness about him that reminded Heather of a bull. Yet he carried no extra weight. His body was hard and athletic, the heavy muscles pressing against the expensive cloth of his suit, as though formal clothes didn't come naturally to him. He was a man made for the outdoor life, riding a horse, surveying his acres, or anything he could do in shirtsleeves.

The champagne was served in tall crystal glasses. Renato raised his in salute. 'To the pleasure of meeting you,' he told Heather.

'To our meeting,' she replied, significantly changing the words. There was the briefest flicker on Renato's face that might have been acknowledgement.

Over cream of cauliflower soup with ribbons of smoked salmon, he talked about Lorenzo and his lengthened visit to England.

'He should have left two weeks ago, but always there are excuses, and I start to understand that some great power is holding him here. And that power comes from a woman. For the first time he is talking about marriage—'

'Renato—' Lorenzo groaned.

'Ignore him,' Heather said. 'He's trying to disconcert you.'

'You seem to understand me by instinct, *signorina*,' Renato said, impressed.

'I don't need instinct. Experience will do. You spent the afternoon trying to disconcert *me*. You like to wrong-foot people.'

He raised his champagne glass in ironic salute, but his eyes, over the rim, were suddenly harder, alert. *'Touché!'* he said. 'I see I shall have to beware of you.'

'What a good idea,' she agreed sweetly. 'Do go on. Lorenzo was talking about marriage and you rushed to England to see if I was good enough.'

'I came to discover if you were as wonderful as he says,' he corrected smoothly. 'And I find that you are.'

It was charmingly said but she wasn't fooled. This was a man who did nothing except for his own reasons. But if he thought she was going to make it easy for him he had another think coming.

'Let's be frank,' she said with a challenging smile. 'Lorenzo is a Martelli. He could marry an heiress. When you found him paying attention to a humble shop assistant it set your alarm bells ringing. That, Signor Martelli, is the truth. The rest is just fancy talk.'

Lorenzo groaned and dropped his head in his hands. Renato reddened slightly. 'Now it is you who are trying to disconcert me.'

'And I'm not doing too badly either,' she murmured.

His response was a grin that blazed out suddenly, taking her by surprise. It was brilliant, intensely masculine, and it came from a fire deep within him.

'Then I too will be frank,' he told her. 'Humble shop assistant! That is nonsense. You feel no more humble than I do. You're a strong woman, even an arrogant one, who thinks she could take on the world, and win. You certainly believe you could get the better of me. You might even be right.'

'Always assuming that I'll need to fight you,' she said lightly. 'But will I?'

'I don't know. I haven't finally decided.'

'I await your decision in fear and trembling,' she told him in an ironic tone that conveyed just the opposite.

He raised his glass in salute. Heather raised hers in return, but she was still on her guard.

'That's the spirit, darling,' Lorenzo said. 'Don't let him scare you.'

'Let her fight her own battles,' Renato told him. 'She's more than capable of it. You see,' he added to Heather, 'I know a lot about you. You left school at sixteen and got a job in a paper shop. For the next four years you went from job to job, always behind a counter, always climbing a little higher, until three years ago you came to work at Gossways.

'You sought a place on their training programme that leads to management, but Gossways refused, saying they take only college graduates. So you set out to prove them wrong. You worked hard, studied languages, badgered them. At last, impressed by your persistence and your splendid sales figures, they gave in, and offered you a place on the next programme. Humble shop assistant! You're a formidable woman.'

'Hey, I didn't know all that,' Lorenzo said.

'Your brother has been asking Gossways Head Office about me,' Heather explained. 'Snooping.'

'Gathering intelligence,' Renato suggested.

'Snooping,' she said firmly. 'And it was very rude.'

'Yes, it was,' Lorenzo said. 'You don't think *I* did anything like that, do you, darling?'

'*You* didn't think of it,' Renato informed him scathingly.

Heather felt a sudden need to get away from the two men, so that she could breathe freely. 'Excuse me, gentlemen,' she said, rising.

She found the powder room and sat gazing at her own reflection in an ornate gilt mirror, wondering why the world always seemed to be the wrong way up. She was being wined and dined at the Ritz, by two attractive men who were giving her their whole attention. That should have made her a woman to be envied, and if she'd been alone with Lorenzo she would have thought so too.

But Renato Martelli made her very, very suspicious.

CHAPTER TWO

WHEN Heather was out of earshot Renato said, 'My compliments. She's charming.'

'You really like her?' Lorenzo asked.

'Yes, I think she's admirable. I admit that I expected a floozy, but she's a *lady*, which must be a first for you. It's time you settled down.'

'Now wait,' Lorenzo said hastily. 'You're rushing me. Why did you tell her I mentioned marriage?'

'Because you did.'

'I said *if* I was thinking about marriage it would be to someone like her. It's a very big step.'

'All the more reason to take it while you're young enough to be influenced by a good woman.'

'*You* didn't.'

Renato gave a wolfish grin. 'Apart from our mother no woman has ever influenced me.'

'That's not what I heard. Wasn't her name Magdalena—? All right, all right,' he finished hastily, looking at his brother's expression.

'Magdalena Conti didn't *influence* me,' Renato said coldly. 'She merely taught me that permanent relationships are not for me. But it's different with you. Beneath your irresponsible ways you have the makings of an excellent husband.'

'Oh, no! I see your game. One of us has to marry and provide a Martelli heir, and you've cast me as the sacrificial lamb. Well, to hell with you, brother! You're the eldest. You do it.'

21

'Forget it. I'm past praying for.'

'And you don't want to give up your nice enjoyable life with all those accommodating ladies,' Lorenzo said indignantly.

'Fidelity has no charms for me,' Renato admitted.

'Why can't Bernardo do the family duty? He's our brother.'

'Our half-brother. He carries our father's blood but not his name, owing to the circumstances of his birth. Besides, he isn't Mamma's son, and his children wouldn't be her grandchildren. No, it has to be one of us, and you're the one who's in love.'

'Yes, but—'

'Hush, she's coming back. Don't be a fool. Make sure of her while you can.'

They rose to greet Heather and Lorenzo kissed her hand. She'd recovered her poise and accepted his tribute with a smile, but inwardly she was still wary.

During the main course a number of visitors came to their table, all of whom eyed Heather curiously, and she began to be self conscious. It was like dipping a toe in shallow water and finding yourself swept away by a tidal wave. Something was happening here that she didn't understand.

At last the visitors had all gone. As Heather was enjoying her chocolate mousse Renato said, 'Lorenzo, I see Felipe di Stefano over there. He's a man you need to speak to.'

When Lorenzo had gone they looked at each other. 'I thought you'd appreciate the chance to tell me exactly what you think of me,' Renato said.

'If I did that we'd be here all night.'

He laughed. 'Go on, say it.'

'Where do I start? Where would it end? Your impertinence in checking up on me with my employers, and then this afternoon—Charles Smith never existed, did he?'

'I'm afraid not.'

'You were *auditioning* me, sizing me up to see if I was "suitable".'

'Certainly I was curious about the woman who's made such an impression on my brother. If I'd told you who I was you wouldn't have acted naturally. I wanted to see you when you weren't trying to impress me.'

'Your conceit is past belief. What makes you think I'd have been trying to impress you?'

'I credit you with enough intelligence to know that you can't marry my brother without impressing me first.'

'Always assuming that I want to marry Lorenzo. I don't think I do, not if it means being related to you.'

'I admit I was a little clumsy. But perhaps you'll forgive me when you hear what I have to say. I admired your behaviour greatly, especially when I abandoned the sale and you lost a large commission. You controlled yourself splendidly.'

'You—did—that—on—purpose?' she breathed.

'Of course. And you passed with flying colours. Lorenzo tends to be emotional and impulsive. Your cool, northern efficiency will be good for him. My congratulations. You've gone the right way to earn my respect.'

'And you're going the right way to earn a chocolate mousse over your head,' she threatened, not in the least appeased by these compliments. 'You actually—you actually—?'

'The lady has finished eating,' Renato said to a waiter, hastily removing her plate with his own hands. 'You may bring the coffee— No—' He corrected himself on seeing the glint in Heather's eyes. 'Best leave the coffee until later.'

When they were alone again he turned to her. 'Please don't be angry. I promise you, the opinion I formed of you was entirely favourable.'

'The opinion that *I* formed of *you* was far from favourable. The things you said to me—'

'I wanted to see if you'd respond to my money—'

'If I was a fortune-hunter!' she snapped.

'The choice of words is yours, but the meaning is the same.'

Heather prided herself on her practical common sense, but this man annoyed her enough to make her toss it aside and take risks instead. The next words seemed to come out of their own accord.

'You'd have looked silly if I'd said yes, wouldn't you?' she said coolly.

'Why? Are you saying that you wouldn't have delivered? I doubt it. I think you're a woman of your word. If you'd promised to sleep with me, you'd have slept with me. We'd have enjoyed a mutually pleasurable experience—'

'*Oh, really?*'

'I promise you it would have been.'

'Perhaps you'd like to give me signed testimonials from Elena and all the other fictitious ladies.'

'They're real enough, and I think they'd vouch for me—although not, perhaps, under these circumstances—'

'At the price you offer I should hope they'd vouch for you under all circumstances. Otherwise they wouldn't be giving what you pay them for, would they?'

That flicked him on the raw, she was glad to notice. His eyes glittered with a strange, dark light. 'Perhaps I've only myself to blame if you sharpen your claws on me,' he said after a moment. 'Let it be. I made you a genuine offer—'

'And never mind what it did to Lorenzo.'

'If you'd accepted I'd have been doing him a favour, and he'd have seen that.'

'People always see things your way, do they?'

'With time and persuasion.'

She regarded him wryly. 'Does that mean that, given time and persuasion, you think you could have seduced me?'

He was suddenly alert. 'I don't know,' he said slowly. 'I simply don't know.'

It was like playing chess, she found, and suddenly very thrilling. Shrewdly she moved her queen into the centre of the board, inviting attack. 'Perhaps you just didn't raise the price high enough,' she murmured.

'What are you saying?'

'Don't you know that a woman who seems honest can charge twice as much as her more blatant sisters?'

'Oh, yes,' he said softly. 'I know that. What now?'

'Come a little nearer, and I'll tell you.'

Slowly he moved his head closer to her. Heather leaned forward until her hair lightly brushed his face, and her breath fanned his cheek.

'I wouldn't want you if you were the last man on earth,' she whispered. *'Go and jump in the river, and take your money with you!'*

He turned his head so that his eyes looked directly into hers. They were hard with astonishment, cold, appraising. 'You are a very unexpected lady,' he said. 'And a very brave one.'

'I don't need to be brave. You can't harm me because you have nothing that I want.'

'Except that I hold your marriage to Lorenzo in my hands. I'm particular about who I take into my family—'

'Then you'll be relieved to know that you won't be

asked to accept me,' she said, drawing back and facing him with furious eyes. 'Let me make my position plain. I hope Lorenzo wasn't planning to propose, because my answer would be no, and *you* are the reason.'

'Heather—' came Lorenzo's dismayed voice from behind her. He had returned in time to hear the last words.

She jumped to her feet. 'I'm sorry, Lorenzo, but it's over. We had a lovely romance but it was just a fairy tale. Now it's reality time, and your reality is your very unpleasant brother.'

He seized her arms. 'Don't go like this. I love you.'

'And I love you, but I'm saying goodbye.'

'Because of *him*? Why?'

'Ask him. Let him tell you if he dares.'

She pulled free and stormed away. Lorenzo started after her but Renato growled, 'Leave this to me.'

Anger gave speed to Heather's feet and she'd already whisked herself halfway down the Long Gallery before Renato had caught up with her.

'This is ridiculous,' he said, reaching for her arm.

'Don't call me ridiculous,' she seethed, shaking him off. 'What's ridiculous is you thinking you can move people like pawns on a chess board.'

'I haven't had much difficulty so far,' he was rash enough to say.

'So I guessed. But you hadn't met me then.'

'Indeed I hadn't—'

'It's been a short acquaintance, not a pleasant one. This is where it ends.'

She turned away sharply and headed for the street. Outside, the night traffic of Piccadilly honked and blared. Renato caught up with her at the door, taking her arm again. 'Please, Heather, come back inside and let's discuss this calmly.'

'I don't feel calm. I feel like throwing something at your head.'

'You're punishing Lorenzo because you're mad at me, and that isn't fair.'

'Not, it's not fair. It's not fair that he has you for a brother, but he's stuck with you. I'm not, however, and I intend to keep it that way.'

'All right, insult me if it gives you pleasure—'

'After the way you've insulted me, it gives me more pleasure than I can say!'

'But don't do this to Lorenzo.'

'I'm doing it *for* Lorenzo. We'd only make each other unhappy. Now, will you please let me go, or do I have to scream for a policeman?'

She pulled free and stormed out onto the pavement, heading straight across the road to where she could see a taxi approaching. She was too angry for caution. Through the noise of the traffic she thought she heard Renato's horrified voice shouting her name. She didn't see the car bearing down on her, only the glare of the headlights against the darkness. Then Renato seized her and swung her violently sideways. Somebody screamed, there was an ugly sound of brakes, and the next moment she was lying in the road.

For a moment she couldn't breathe. But she didn't seem to be injured. A crowd was gathering around her, hands outstretched. Lorenzo burst through, crying, 'Heather, my God! *Oh, my God!*'

His voice rose on a note of horror and she realised that he wasn't looking at her but at his brother. Renato lay in the road, bleeding from a wound in his arm. With a terrible sick feeling Heather saw why Lorenzo had cried out. Renato looked as though he'd severed an artery. Blood was streaming from his arm in a river, and if something wasn't done fast he had little time left.

'Give me your tie,' she told Lorenzo. 'Quickly!'

He wrenched it off, while she fumbled in her bag for her pen. Her head was spinning but she fought to clear it while her hands moved swiftly, wrapping the tie around Renato's arm above the wound, knotting it, slipping the pen through and twisting it. Renato's eyes were open and he was looking at her, but she tried to think of nothing but what she was doing, twisting, twisting, while the tourniquet around his arm grew tighter and tighter, until at last—oh, thank God!—the bleeding lessened and stopped as the vein was closed.

'Lorenzo—' she gasped.

'Yes,' he said, taking the tourniquet from her. 'I'll hold it now.'

'Thank you—I'm feeling a little—' Her head was swimming.

'No, you're not going to faint,' Renato murmured.

'Aren't I?'

'A woman like you doesn't faint. She takes over and gives orders, but she never weakens.' His voice was almost inaudible, but she heard every word.

'Let us through, please.'

Suddenly an ambulance was there, the crew urging their way through the crowd, taking over. There were police too, talking to the motorist who was wringing his hands and protesting his innocence. Heather forced her head to clear. She still had something to do.

'It wasn't his fault,' she said urgently to the policeman. 'I ran out in front of him.'

'All right, miss, we'll talk at the hospital,' the young constable said.

Lorenzo helped her into the ambulance and sat beside

her, pulling off his jacket and wrapping it around her, warming her against the shock. Renato presented a ghastly sight, covered in blood and with a pallor on his face that suggested death hadn't been far off. One of the crew was giving him oxygen, and at last he opened his eyes over the mask. His gaze wandered to Heather, then to Lorenzo. His expression was intent, as though he were sending a silent message to one of them. Or perhaps both.

At the hospital Renato was hurried away for emergency treatment, while Heather's grazes were tended. She emerged to find Lorenzo sitting in the corridor with two policemen. She repeated what she'd said before, exonerating the driver. At last they left, satisfied, and she could be alone with Lorenzo.

He put his arms about her. 'Are you all right, darling?'

'Yes, it was just scratches. What about Renato?'

'He's in there.' He indicated the opposite door. 'They've stopped the bleeding and given him a transfusion. He's got to stay here a few days, but he's going to be all right.'

A doctor emerged. 'You can come in for a minute. Just one of you.'

'I'm his brother,' Lorenzo said, 'but this is my fiancée—please.'

'All right, but try to be quiet.'

Renato looked less alarming without his blood-stained clothes, but still very pale. He was lying with his eyes closed, not moving but for the light rise and fall of his chest.

'I've never seen him this still,' Lorenzo said. 'Usually he's striding about, giving orders. What did he say to make you storm out like that?'

'I can hardly remember. Whatever it was, I shouldn't have put his life in danger.'

'I only know that he was bleeding to death and you saved him. Thank you, *amor mia*. I know he can be a bear, but he's a good fellow really. Thank God you were there!'

'If I hadn't been there it wouldn't have happened,' she said, touched by his belief in her, but feeling guilty at the same time.

Lorenzo slipped an arm about her shoulders. She rested her head against him and they sat together, exchanging warmth and comfort.

'Are you angry that I called you my fiancée?' he asked after a while.

'No, I'm not angry.'

'Do you love me enough to forgive Renato, and take me on?'

Renato's eyes had opened and he was watching them. 'Say yes,' he urged her. 'Don't turn us down.'

'Us?'

'If you marry one Martelli, you get the whole pack of us.'

'I'll be a good husband,' Lorenzo vowed. 'Good enough to make up for Renato.'

'What more do you need to hear than that?' Renato asked.

'Nothing,' she said with a smile. 'I guess I can take the risk!'

Suddenly everything was happening fast. The traumatic evening had swept her up in a fierce tide of emotion, and under its influence she'd promised to marry Lorenzo.

In an instant, it seemed she was part of the Martelli family. Renato had stretched out his good hand and clasped hers, weakly, but with warmth. 'Now I shall have a sister.'

Within twenty-four hours her left hand bore a ring with a large diamond. Two days later she saw the brothers off from Heathrow Airport, knowing that her own ticket was booked for a month ahead.

Now she was on the flight to Palermo, still wondering what had come over her. Beside her sat Dr Angela Wenham: Angie, her closest friend and flatmate, who was enjoying a well-earned holiday.

'I'm so glad you asked me to come with you as brides-maid,' Angie said now. 'I'm looking forward to a few days just living for pleasure.'

Besides being brainy and hard working Angie was also pretty, daintily built, and a social butterfly. Her recent stint on hospital night duty had severely restricted her romantic life, and she was intent on making up for it, if the smile on her delightful, impish face was anything to go by.

'Fancy you being swept off your feet,' Angie chuckled 'Much more my style than yours.'

'Yes, it's not like sturdy, dependable me, is it?' Heather mused. 'And the way I acted that night—I swear I didn't know myself. Normally I'm a quiet sort of person, but I was ranting and raving, telling him where to get off—'

Angie collapsed with laughter. '*You?* Ranting and raving? How I wish I'd been there to see that!'

'I swear it's true. I even told him I disliked him enough to turn Lorenzo down.'

'Wasn't that true?'

'No, it wasn't. But he got me so mad I said the first thing that came into my head.'

Angie looked mischievous. 'You did say he had two brothers, didn't you?'

'You're incorrigible,' Heather laughed. 'I've only met Renato.'

'Ah, yes, the monster Renato.'

'I have to be fair. He's not a monster. I was mad at the way he inspected me, but he could have died because of me. He's welcomed me into the family, and he actually restored his cancelled order afterwards. Someone turned up from the Ritz and collected it.'

'Tell me about the other one.'

'There's also a half-brother, called Bernardo. Their father had an affair with a woman from one of the mountain villages, and Bernardo was their son. They were together in the car crash that killed them both, and Lorenzo's mother took the boy in and raised him with her own sons.'

'What an incredible woman!'

'I know. Her name's Baptista, and if I'm worried about anything, it's how she's going to view me.'

'But you showed me the letter she wrote you. It was lovely.'

'It's just that someone who can put her own feelings aside to do what she saw as her duty—well, you'd never really know what she was thinking, would you?'

'It's what Lorenzo thinks about you that counts,' Angie said staunchly. 'Hey, isn't that Sicily, down there?'

From here they could see the triangular island: close to Italy, yet apart from it, separated only by a narrow strip of water, the Straits of Messina, yet with its own distinct identity.

'A Sicilian,' Lorenzo had told her, 'is always a Sicilian first and an Italian afterwards. Sometimes he is barely an Italian at all. So many races meet in us that we think of ourselves as a race apart, doing things our own way.'

She was searching for him as soon as she and Angie left Customs. And there he was, with another man. He waved eagerly to her and broke into a run. Heather hastened towards him, while Angie brought up the rear, smiling, pushing the baggage trolley, and eyeing the second man with pleasurable speculation.

Lorenzo hugged his bride, kissing her between words. 'It's been such—a long—time, my darling.'

'Yes—yes,' she said kissing him back.

It was marvellous how certain she was now that she was here. Within a few minutes of landing in Sicily Heather knew she had come home. Everything about this place felt perfect, even before she'd discovered the details. And that could only mean that she was doing the right thing in marrying Lorenzo.

'This is my brother, Bernardo,' Lorenzo said at last, indicating the man with him.

'Half-brother,' murmured the man.

'Bernardo, meet Heather, my bride-to-be.'

She introduced Angie to Lorenzo. But when he tried to present Bernardo his brother waved him away with a grin. 'We've already introduced ourselves,' he said, 'while you two were—er—saying hello.'

This caused general laughter. Bernardo took charge of the trolley and they made their way to the car, where he invited Angie to sit in the front with him.

'They won't want to be disturbed,' he said, smiling.

So many sensations were converging on Heather that she had only a confused impression of the most brilliant colours she had ever seen, the bluest sky, the sweetest air. Bernardo swung the car around the outskirts of Palermo and down the coast, and soon the Residenza Martelli came into sight.

Heather sat up to watch it eagerly. Lorenzo had told her about his home, how it was built on an incline, over-looking the sea, but no words had conveyed its beauty. It rose before them, tier upon tier, balcony on balcony, each one a sea of blooms. Geraniums, jasmine, white and red oleanders, clematis and bougainvillaea danced together in a dizzying riot of colour that was always in perfect harmony.

Then they were on a winding road that twisted and turned, bringing the villa nearer until at last they swung into a courtyard. A flight of broad steps led up to a wide, arched entrance, with a door that was being opened from the inside. Through it came a small, elderly woman, making her way slowly with the aid of a walking stick. She took her place on the top step.

'That's my mother,' Lorenzo said, taking Heather's hand to lead her up the stairs.

Baptista looked imperious, despite her evident frailty and the fact that she barely came up to Lorenzo's shoulder. She was in her early sixties, but illness had aged her and she looked older. Beneath her shining white hair her face was sharp, and her brilliant blue eyes missed nothing. But Heather saw the warmth in those eyes, and when the thin arms went around her she felt the unexpected strength in the old woman's embrace.

'Welcome, my dear,' Baptista said. 'Welcome to the family.'

She was beaming, her expression full of kindness. She greeted Angie equally warmly. 'When you have seen your room, then we can take a little refreshment together.'

Although the house bore the modest title of Residenza, it might more aptly have been called a palace. It was built in medieval style, of beautiful yellow stone, with long tile and mosaic corridors. The rooms were lined sometimes with marble, sometimes with tapestries. Everywhere Heather saw wealth, beauty, elegance, and an inbred assumption of authority.

She and Angie were sharing a huge room. It bore two large four-poster beds hung with white net curtains which matched those at the tall windows leading onto the broad terrace, facing inland. Beneath it was the huge garden, and beyond that the land stretched away until it rose into dark, misty mountains on the horizon. Everywhere the colours had a vividness Heather had never seen before. After the pastel shades of England their sheer depth and brightness overwhelmed her.

A maid helped them unpack, then showed them out onto the terrace that went all around the house, and led them to the front, where Baptista was seated at a small rustic table, looking out over the bay. Bernardo and Lorenzo were there, and immediately drew out chairs, and when they were seated filled their glasses with Marsala. A larger table nearby was laden with Sicilian cheesecake, zabaglione, coffee ice with whipped cream, candied fruit ring, and several other things that they were too dazed to take in.

'I wasn't sure of your preferences, so I ordered a variety,' Baptista murmured.

The food and wine were delicious. Overhead a flowered awning sheltered them from the bright sun, and a soft breeze was springing up. Heather wondered how she had ever lived before coming to this perfect place. Lorenzo kept catching her eye and smiling, and his smile was irresistible, making her return it.

'That's enough,' Baptista said imperiously, tapping his hand. 'You'll have plenty of time to play the fool, my son. Go away now, and let me get to know your bride.'

CHAPTER THREE

WHEN Lorenzo had vanished, and Bernardo was showing Angie the garden, Baptista refilled Heather's glass. 'Renato told me how your prompt action saved his life,' she said. 'You and I have been friends from that moment.'

'You're very kind,' Heather said, 'but didn't he also tell you that it was my fault he was ever in danger?'

'I think he was largely to blame. He made you angry with his high-handedness. I've spoken to him very severely.'

Heather concealed a smile. The idea of the domineering Renato being alarmed by anything his frail mother might say was charming, but unconvincing.

'You are going to be very important to this family,' Baptista continued. 'More important than perhaps you can imagine. Lorenzo says you have no family of your own.'

'I was an only child. My mother died when I was six. My father couldn't cope without her.' Heather paused. She seldom talked about this because it seemed a betrayal of the sweet-natured, confused little man who'd longed only to follow his wife. But suddenly she wanted to confide in Baptista. 'He drank rather more than he ought,' she said. 'In the end he couldn't keep a job.'

'And so you looked after him,' Baptista said gently.

'We sort of looked after each other. He was kind and I loved him. When I was sixteen he caught pneumonia and just faded away. The last thing he said to me was, "Sorry, love."'

She'd sobbed over her father's grave, unable to voice

36

the real pain: the knowledge that she hadn't been enough for him. The practical difficulties had followed—lack of money, the abandonment of her dream of college, seizing the first job she could find. She explained in as few words as possible, and had the feeling that Baptista understood.

They talked for an hour, and each moment Heather felt herself grow closer to this regal but kindly woman. When Lorenzo poked his head out through the net curtains with a questioning look on his face, both women welcomed him with a smile. Laughing, he joined them, bringing fresh cakes.

From inside the house they heard Renato's voice, and suddenly he appeared through the long white curtains. When she'd seen him and Lorenzo off at the airport in England he'd looked pale, his arm in a sling. Now he moved freely and his look of vibrant health had returned.

She felt a slight shock. She had forgotten his massiveness, the heavy muscles of his neck, his air of being about to charge. Here in his native land, amid the fierce sun and the bright colours, that effect was reinforced.

Renato went first to his mother, greeting her with a mixture of affection and respect that caught Heather's attention. Then he turned to her.

'Welcome to my sister,' he said, placing a hand lightly on her shoulder and kissing her cheek. She had a moment's intense awareness of his spicy male scent. Then he moved away and greeted Lorenzo with a mock punch to the chin. Lorenzo returned the compliment and for a moment the two brothers engaged in a light-hearted tussle, as lively as young stallions, their voices rich with laughter. It ended with them thumping each other on the back in a way that suggested their mutual affection.

Baptista met Heather's eye, inviting her to share her pride and pleasure in her magnificent sons. Heather nodded, thinking that one day it would be her turn. At least, she hoped so.

At last Renato seated himself opposite her, smiling self-consciously. He was dressed informally, in fawn trousers and a short-sleeved shirt. Against the white material his skin, tanned to dark brown, showed up sharply. His black hair was tousled, and grew more so when he ran his hand through it after brushing the damp from his forehead. Heather had the feeling that everything else had grown pale. Just by being there, leaning back, half sprawled in his chair, he made everything revolve around him.

The light was fading. Someone asked where Bernardo and Angie were, and Lorenzo went to find them, amid good-natured laughter. Heather recalled Angie's laughing words on the plane, and hoped her friend hadn't been carried away by her impulsive romantic tendencies.

When it was time to get ready for dinner Heather went to her room and Angie appeared a moment later, her eyes shining. 'Have a nice time?' Heather asked.

'Lovely, thank you,' Angie said with suspicious innocence.

Just as they finished dressing there was a knock on the door and Baptista swept regally in, carrying a black box.

'Perfect,' she said, smiling at the wedding dress which Heather had set up on a stand near the window. 'And this will go with it.' She opened the box, revealing a tiara made of flawless pearls. 'Legend says that it once adorned the head of Queen Marie Antoinette,' she said. 'Later it passed to the Martelli family, and for generations it has been given to a bride for her wedding veil.'

'But—it's kind of you—but this is too much for me. What about when Renato marries? Won't he expect—?'

'That is no matter,' Baptista observed imperiously. 'If

he's so stupid and stubborn about marriage he has only himself to blame. Come, try it on.'

The tiara was perfect when set on Heather's luxuriant fair hair, but best of all was the way Baptista accepted her. She thanked her but was relieved when Baptista offered to keep the jewels in her safe until the wedding.

Seeing the glories of the Residenza, Heather was glad she'd splashed out on some expensive clothes—or, at least, they would have been expensive if she hadn't bought them at Gossways, heavily discounted. She was popular, and friends on many floors had slashed prices to the bone for her.

As a result she was able to appear in the medieval dining room in an off-the-shoulder pale yellow silk that followed the contours of her body without being obviously seductive. For sheer splendour she was outdone by Angie, a sizzling peacock in blues and greens that seemed almost to flame. But Lorenzo had eyes only for her, and Renato too seemed struck by the sight of her.

Baptista took her by the hand and led her forward, saying, 'Here is our guest of honour,' to be introduced to some local dignitaries. Then she was seated at the head of the table, between Lorenzo and Baptista, becoming uneasily aware that everyone was deferring to her, like a queen.

It was delightful but it made her nervous to have every dish presented for her approval. The meal was practically a banquet, and Baptista explained that the kitchen was practising for the wedding reception. The finest Sicilian cuisine was on offer. To start with, a choice of stuffed baked tomatoes, orange salad, stuffed rice ball fritters, bean fritters. Then the rice and pasta dishes, Sicilian rice, rice with artichokes, pasta with sardines, pasta with cauliflower, and the main dishes still to come.

By the time they reached the braised lamb, stuffed beef roll, and rabbit in sweet and sour sauce Heather was running out of appetite. But she knew that to say so would cause offence to those who had laboured to bring forth this feast in her honour, so she ploughed on valiantly.

'Perhaps you would rather have no more,' Baptista suggested gently, seeming to understand.

'But I must try those sweet dishes,' Heather said. 'They look so delicious.'

Watermelon jelly, fried pastries with ricotta cheese and candied fruit, pistachio cakes, nougat—she took a mouthful of each, and was rewarded by the looks of approval from every direction.

But the reward that touched her heart the most was when Baptista whispered, 'Well done, my daughter.'

She couldn't help being struck by the three brothers. All elegantly dressed in dinner jackets, they made an impressive sight: Lorenzo, the tallest, the most handsome; Bernardo, lean and dark with a gravity that made his rare smiles breathtaking—and Renato, dour, forceful, with his air of giving no quarter and asking none. He would be a difficult man to get to know, she thought, despite his evident intention of making her welcome.

Twice during the meal Renato was summoned from the table to take a phone call. In the gathering that followed Angie murmured, 'Bernardo says that Renato is the worker of the family and Lorenzo the charmer.'

'And what is Bernardo?' Heather wanted to know.

Angie's eyes twinkled. 'Tell you later.'

As the guests began to leave Lorenzo took her hand, whispering, 'Come with me,' and drawing her out of the room.

Hand in hand they ran up the stairs and along a corri-

dor, until he reached a pair of oak double doors. He flung
them open, revealing a large austerely beautiful room,
hung with tapestries. 'There are going to be three uncles
sleeping in this room,' he said. 'But after that—oh, come
here!'

He pulled her into his arms and in the tenderness of his
kiss she forgot everything else. It felt so good to be here,
knowing that she'd come home.

'Excuse me,' came a voice from behind them. They
jumped apart and saw Renato in the doorway, grinning.
'Sorry to disturb you,' he said. 'How do you like your
apartment?'

'Our what?'

'This set of rooms is almost self-contained,' Lorenzo
explained. 'It would be just perfect for us.'

'You mean—live here, instead of having a home of our
own?' Heather asked, dismayed.

'But this *will* be a home of our own.'

'No, it won't. We'll be right next to your brother.'

'A terrible fate,' Renato agreed.

'It's nothing personal—' she started to say.

'Oh, I think it is,' he said, meeting her eyes.

'If we're here, Lorenzo will be at your beck and call.
I dare say that's how you prefer it—'

'But will you have time to arrange a house before you
marry in just over a week?' Renato asked reasonably. 'Of
course Lorenzo could have chosen something already, but
I thought you'd prefer to do that yourself. Why do you
assume the worst of me?'

'Instinct,' she said, not mincing matters.

He grinned, unashamed. 'You wrong me.'

'No, I don't.' But she couldn't help smiling back at
him. He was a devil, but he could be a disastrously en-
gaging devil.

'You can start househunting later,' Renato assured her. 'Meanwhile, these rooms will be comfortable.'

It all sounded so reasonable, but her warning signals were flashing. Renato liked to keep people where he wanted them, and sounding reasonable was just another way of doing it. His teasing look showed that he followed her thought processes perfectly.

'Just for a little while, then,' she said at last. 'As soon as we return from honeymoon—'

'Not quite that soon,' Renato said. 'Lorenzo has a trip scheduled for New York—'

'Oh, really—' she began, up in arms again.

'And I naturally assumed that you'd want to go with him.'

Her weapons clattered uselessly to the floor. She would die for a trip to New York.

'That only leaves your honeymoon,' Renato said.

'Don't tell me you've arranged that too!'

'I thought you might borrow my boat for a couple of weeks' cruising. The crew will do the work; all you need do is enjoy yourself.'

'It's a beautiful boat, darling,' Lorenzo broke in eagerly. 'A sloop, with air-conditioning and—'

'And the two of you have settled it. Suppose I don't like sailing? Suppose I get seasick?'

'Do you?' Renato enquired.

'I don't know. I've never been on a boat.'

'Then the sooner you do, the better. Tomorrow Lorenzo has to go to Stockholm, to catch up on his delayed schedule. I shall take you out on the boat and you can let me know your decision.'

Heather had half expected Angie to come with them on the boat trip, but she was spending the day with Bernardo.

'He's going to show me his home village in the mountains.'

'You only met him yesterday,' Heather protested.

'I know.' Angie's chuckle was full of delight.

'You be careful.'

But Angie glowed with the self-confidence of a young woman who'd always been able to win any man she chose. She laughed merrily, and a moment later Heather heard her singing in the shower.

There was no mistaking the *Santa Maria*, a beautiful single-masted boat, over a hundred feet long, dominating everything in the little harbour of Mondello. Renato parked the car and handed her out. 'What do you think of her?' he asked in a voice full of love and pride.

'She's lovely,' Heather admitted.

He leapt lightly down onto the deck and reached up to settle both hands about her waist. The next moment she was swinging through the air to land beside him. 'All right?' he asked.

'Yes,' she said breathlessly. The sudden movement had taken her by surprise.

He introduced the crew, who were lined up to greet her.

'This is Alfonso, my captain, Gianni and Carlo, the crew. And this,' he added, indicating a little man, 'is Fredo the cook. He can manage anything from the fastest snacks to *cordon bleu*.'

The sun was bright and warm, a strong breeze whisked across the water, and soon they were edging out of the harbour into the wide sea beyond. After a few minutes Heather became used to the movement, and even began to find it pleasant.

'Well?' Renato asked, watching her face. 'Do you want

to go back, throw yourself overboard, throw *me* over-board—?'

'That last one sounds nice,' she said, laughing.

He shared her laughter, showing strong white teeth against his tanned skin. After the tense, argumentative man she'd met in England, this was a transformation. His clothes, too, were different. The elegant formality of last night was replaced by blue shorts and a white short-sleeved shirt, that was unbuttoned all the way. He looked powerful, glowing with life, intensely masculine.

'Let me show you your kingdom,' Renato said, taking her hand.

Below, it was like a little palace. In the galley Fredo, surrounded by the most modern equipment, was furiously at work on a feast. Along the narrow corridor was the master bedroom, complete with luxurious private bath-room. Everywhere was panelled with gleaming honey-coloured birchwood. At the centre was a huge double bed, the perfect place for lovers on their wedding night.

'This is yours for today,' Renato told her. 'Why not change into a swimsuit?'

'I don't even own one.'

He pulled open a wardrobe to display a series of swim-suits on hangers. Heather stared. There must have been about ten, in all colours, styles, and varying degrees of daringness.

'But how come you—?' She checked as she saw the wicked humour in his eyes. 'I'm not even going to ask.'

'You don't really need to, do you?' he asked.

His sexuality was so frank, his appetites so shameless that she didn't know where to look. She began to rifle through some pastel-coloured costumes, but Renato's big hand came out of nowhere and stilled hers.

'Not those,' he said. 'This one.'

He held up a bikini but she instinctively shook her head. 'No, I can't—'

'Why not? It's very modest.'

That was true. As bikinis went it was unfashionably modest. The lower part would cover most of her behind, and the upper part would enclose her breasts satisfactorily. But Heather had always seen herself as a once-piece person.

'And I can't wear cerise,' she argued. 'I'm too fair.'

'There's no law to stop you wearing reds. Risk it.'

'Right, I will.'

When he'd gone she changed, realising that in this place the dramatic colour seemed natural. She found a matching scarf in the wardrobe and tied it around her head, letting her hair fall free behind it. To cover her semi-nakedness she slipped on a robe of white lacy silk.

Back on deck she found Renato in the stern section, with a table that bore snacks and tall glasses. Above him a striped awning offered shelter from the sun. He handed her gallantly to her seat, and served her. The chilled wine was delicious; the little almond cakes were superb. Heather began to feel that she could easily get used to this.

'Sicily's at the centre of the Mediterranean,' Renato explained. 'So the boat can take you anywhere, easily. You can go across to Tunisia, or head the other way to Greece, or sail up the coast of Italy.'

'Where are we going today?'

'Just part of the way around the island, and then back. We'll find a quiet bay, take a swim. Are you feeling seasick yet?'

'Not at all,' she admitted. 'In fact, it feels wonderful.' She took a deep breath of salty air. 'Mmm!'

He grinned. 'We'll make a sailor of you yet.'

They toasted each other and she ate some of the little marzipan fruits, which looked so perfect that at first she thought they were the real thing. Then Renato took the helm and she stood beside him with the wind in her hair and the soft mist of water in her face, suddenly possessed by happiness and well-being.

'Why not sunbathe?' he suggested. 'But first rub in some sun cream—your skin is very fair and you must protect it.'

'The sun never touches me,' she said, a little regretfully.

'English sun,' Renato said dismissively. 'What do you know of the heat in my country? Even on land it can be fierce, but here the water reflects the sun back and doubles its strength. There's sun block in your cabin.'

She chose one of the luxurious lotions in her little bathroom, and went back up on deck to stretch out. Renato watched as she smoothed the silky liquid over her arms and legs. 'Turn over and let me do your back,' he said. 'Think how my brother would blame me if you went to your wedding looking like a lobster! I tremble at the prospect.'

'Tremble?' she chuckled. 'You?'

'I assure you that under this grim exterior beats the heart of a mouse.'

She gave in and rolled over onto her stomach. The touch of Renato's fingertips on her spine was unexpectedly light, not forceful, but almost delicate. She rested her head on her hands and began to relax as he worked on the back of her neck, kneading the cream in thoroughly with both hands.

Through half-closed eyes she watched the sun slanting on the deck. The hypnotic rhythm of his hands, strong yet sensitive, was making the edges of the world blur, so that she couldn't tell where one thing ended and another began, or where she ended and the world began. The blood was pulsing slowly, blissfully through her veins...

Suddenly she was awake, forcing herself back to reality through clouds of contented sensation. Somewhere there were seagulls calling, the waves lashing noisily against the side of the boat, but her heart was beating so loudly that it blotted out these sounds. She turned sharply and found Renato looking at her with something in his eyes that might have been shock.

'I must return to the helm,' he said, his voice coming from a long way off.

'Yes,' she replied vaguely. 'You must.'

To her relief he left her. She looked around, finding to her surprise that everything was in its normal place. Her heart was pounding, but gradually it slowed to a soft throb of pleasure. She was breathless, as though she'd been running. And Renato had been the same, she recalled. She lay down again, meaning to puzzle it out, but contentment overcame her, and a moment later she was asleep.

Renato's light touch on her shoulder awoke her. 'We've dropped anchor,' he said. 'Just over there is a little bay.'

The *Santa Maria* had a small dinghy, already loaded with a picnic hamper and being lowered to the water. Renato handed her into it and they were away, headed for a small golden beach where there was nobody else in sight.

'Let's swim before we eat,' he suggested. 'Come.' He seized her hand and they ran down the yellow sand.

The shock of the cool water was delicious. She plunged in and together they swam out to deep water. She'd never swum so far from shore before, and she wasn't a strong swimmer, but she felt full of confidence as long as Renato was there. They swam for half an hour, then headed back, side by side.

'Let's stay in a bit longer,' he said as their feet touched ground.

'No, I'll unpack the picnic. You go back if you want another swim.'

He raced away and plunged back into the water while she dried off her hair, and swung it in the sun for a moment. When she looked out to sea again he'd vanished. The water was clear and level, and there wasn't a sign of Renato.

Slowly she got to her feet, feeling as though a dark cloud had covered the sun. It was like waking in a lunar landscape where everything was bare and desolate, and no life would ever live again.

Then his head broke the surface and the world was bathed in her relief. He waved and she waved back, discovering that she'd been holding her breath.

'You scared me,' she accused him as he walked up the beach.

He grinned. 'Sorry. I like to swim under water for as long as I can.'

He towelled himself dry, and sat down beside her. The movement gave her a good view of the ugly scar near his wrist, and she shuddered.

'It's nothing,' he said. 'It's healed. See.'

He held out his hand and she took it between hers, turning it to see the scar better. As he'd said, it had healed beautifully, but now she saw how large the wound had been, how close he had come to death. His big, forceful hand looked strange against her slim, delicate ones. By tightening it he could have crushed her, but he let it lie there while she gently brushed the sand from it.

'I always said no woman would ever leave a permanent mark on me,' he mused. 'But now one has.'

'It's not really funny.' Something inside her chest was aching.

'All right, then I'll tell you something serious. What happened that night told me all about you. One minute you were telling me to jump in the river. The next you were saving my life as cool as a cucumber, despite having been knocked about yourself. And when you did weaken, just a little, you pulled yourself together so that you could clear the driver.'

'That's my English reserve and efficiency,' she teased. 'We're well known for keeping our cool.'

'Does anything throw you off balance?'

'Probably nothing you could think of,' she said with a smile.

'By God, I did the right thing bringing you here!' he said suddenly.

'You? It was Lorenzo who brought me here.'

'Of course, of course. I think we should eat now.'

The picnic was magnificent and Renato explained that Fredo had outdone himself in her honour. As they sipped the cool wine, the slight movement of his face drew her attention to another scar. It made him look as though he'd tangled with a wild animal and emerged battered. She wondered how the animal would look. He caught her gaze and he rubbed it self consciously.

'I'm sorry,' she said, horrified at herself.

He shrugged. 'It makes no difference. Nature didn't make me a beauty to start with. Then I played the fool on a motorbike and got what I deserved.'

'You did that on a motorbike?'

'I was wild as a boy. I bought a fast bike and rode it to the limit. The police warned me time and again, but I was a Martelli and that has its privileges. Then I took a mountain bend at an insane speed and nearly killed myself. Luckily nobody else got hurt, and I was left with this scar on my face as a reminder not to be a damned fool.'

'I can't picture you wild, somehow. You seem so much in control.'

'I learned the consequences of not being in control the hard way. Besides, my father was dead by then, and the firm was being run by an uncle who wasn't very good at it. Somebody had to get a grip while there was still time.'

'So the firm had to become your life?'

'It's a more useful life than dashing about getting myself half killed. And now I find it very satisfying.'

She noticed that 'now' and wondered how hard it had been for a young man addicted to excitement to put on a suit and chain himself to a desk.

He said casually, 'My mother told me that you were reluctant to accept her gift yesterday.'

'The pearl tiara, yes. It's a family heirloom. You're the eldest son. Surely it should go to your wife?'

'Who doesn't exist, and never will. The single life suits me too well to give up.'

'Oh, yes, Elena, Julia and the rest of the crowd. I don't believe it. It sounds so immature, and I don't think you *are* immature.'

He grimaced wryly. 'I didn't always feel this way. There was a lady once—her name was Magdalena Conti—the story is nauseatingly sentimental. I was much younger, and I believed in things I don't believe in now. She taught me a lesson in reality from which I benefited enormously.'

'Is she why you think all women are fortune-hunters?'

He shrugged. 'Possibly. She was beautiful, tender, loving. She was also greedy, manipulative and deadly. She aimed her arrows at me for money. I fell for it. She told me she was pregnant. I asked her to marry me. I'd have asked her anyway, but fatherhood thrilled me. I indulged in many dreams in those days.'

He fell silent, looking out over the sea. His eyes might have been fixed on the horizon, or maybe on some other horizon, inside himself.

'And then?' Heather asked softly.

'Then she met another man, much richer, and in films, which she found exciting. At our final meeting I learned for the first time how much I bored her. Then she went off with him.'

'And your baby?'

'She never gave birth. I know that much. Perhaps the child was an invention, or perhaps she—' He shrugged. 'I prefer to think she was lying about the pregnancy, but the truth is that I shall never know.'

Heather was silent. There was nothing she could have said that wouldn't have sounded like a mockery of his pain. And the pain was unmistakable, even after so long. Suddenly the air about her was jagged with suffering. At the same time she was wondering about the woman who could be bored by this man.

'Now the only woman I trust is my mother,' he finished. 'Lorenzo is fortunate to have found you.'

'So you think I can be trusted? Then surely, other women can?'

'Lorenzo still knows how to *give* trust. But I don't. I would invite betrayal by expecting it, and—forgive me— such expectations are always fulfilled in the end. I made my decision, and I'll stick to it. Take my mother's gift. No woman will ever challenge you for it.'

She refilled his glass and he accepted it with a slightly forced smile.

'Do you think you'll be happy here, Heather?' he asked quietly.

'I've known it from the first moment. It's not like me to be so impulsive, but Lorenzo made me feel so wanted.'

He looked at her intently. 'Had nobody ever made you feel that way before?'

'There was someone else, quite recently. We were engaged for a year, and he called it all off a week before the wedding. I suppose it left me feeling a bit bruised and rejected.'

Then a dreadful thought occurred to her. 'But don't think I accepted Lorenzo on the rebound. It's not just because of Peter. It's Lorenzo himself, the way he is—so loving and warm-hearted.'

To her surprise Renato was frowning as though something troubled him deeply. At last he said, 'Heather, if ever you're in trouble, promise that you will come to me.'

'But why should I when I can go to him?'

'He's a fine fellow, but if you need an older brother's help, please remember that I'm here.'

She would have turned the moment aside with a laugh, but something in Renato's manner stopped her. There was a strange intensity in his eyes.

'Promise me, *miu soru*,' he urged.

'What was that you called me?'

'*Miu soru*. It's Sicilian. It means, "my sister", for that's what you must be now.'

'And what is "my brother"?'

'*Miu frati*. Promise your brother. Give him your word.'

There was something in his urgency that was as puzzling as his frown had been. 'All right, I promise,' she said. '*Miu frati*.'

'Shake?'

'Shake.' Her hand was engulfed in his big one, and for

a moment she could feel the power flowing through him, power that he'd just offered to put at her service.

'And to show that I'm really your brother,' he added, 'may I give you away at your wedding?'

She was touched. 'Thank you. That's very kind.'

'For my sister, nothing is too much,' he said gravely, raising her hand and brushing his lips against the back of it. Suddenly a stillness came over both of them. It was so total that Heather could hear and feel her heart thumping. She had the odd sensation that the whole world was pulsing with it.

Abruptly, he released her hand. Heather stared at it, wondering what had happened. Why did she have this strange feeling that the world had changed, that the sun had grown dark and the heat more intense?

'We should go back now.' Renato's voice was strange.

'Yes,' she replied, not knowing what she said.

But by the time they'd packed everything into the dinghy the brief sensation had passed and she was chiding herself for imagining things. The whole Martelli family had opened their arms to her in welcome, and the sensation was so unfamiliar that it was distorting her perceptions. As the little boat sped across the water the rushing wind blew the last crazy thoughts from her head.

CHAPTER FOUR

ON THE journey home Heather took a fascinated look at the stern, where a jet ski, big enough for two people, was fixed.

'Would you care to try it?' Renato asked.

'I'd love to,' she said eagerly.

Slowly the jet ski was winched down to the water. Renato leapt down and took the front seat, and Heather eased her way into the seat behind him. She had just time to wrap her arms about him before they roared away across the water. The speed, noise and vibration took her by surprise and she tightened her arms, turning her head sideways and pressing herself against Renato's broad back.

'*All right?*' Renato roared back at her.

She could barely make out the words through the noise, but she yelled back, '*Fine!*'

It was true. The vibration was taking her over, coming up through every part of her flesh, her thighs, her stomach, her breasts where they were pressed against Renato's back. The water rushed by, lashing her with white foam, whipping up her excitement in the most physically exhilarating experience of her life. Renato's body was like a strong column in her arms. She clung onto him, eyes closed, relishing his warmth.

At last he slowed and brought the jet ski to a halt.

'*Wahooo!*' she cried.

'You enjoyed it, then?' he said, turning his head and grinning at her.

'Oh, yes!' she said happily. 'Oh, yes, I did! Where are

we?' She caught sight of the boat, which looked tiny in the distance. 'It's miles away.'

'These things travel very fast. Another few minutes and we'd have been out of sight of the boat.'

A mad impulse seized her. 'Let's!'

'You want to go on?'

'And on and on and on!' she cried out, throwing her head back and carolling up to the sky.

'Heather, what's got into you?' He was laughing, but he sounded half alarmed at something wild and uncontrolled about her.

'Nothing. Everything. The whole world!'

'I think we should go back.'

'Never. I want to go forward. Start her up.'

'Right!' Something he'd heard in her voice got to him and he kicked the engine into life, swinging away towards the horizon, then driving forward across the endless water.

Soon the *Santa Maria* was out of sight. For some reason Heather found that knowledge thrilling, as though she had cut loose from all safety and restraint in a way she'd never felt able to do in her life before. The sense of freedom was mindblowing. She unwrapped her arms from Renato's body and rested her hands lightly on his shoulders. Now she felt quite safe this way. She was invincible. Nothing could happen to her.

But the next moment they swerved sharply. Caught off guard, she tried to grip his shoulders more tightly, but it was too late. There was nothing to hold onto, and then she was flying through the air to land in the water with a crash.

At this speed it was like slamming into a brick wall. For a dreadful moment everything went black. She was half unconscious, sinking, sinking into the depths that went on for ever, and the horror was engulfing her. Somehow she managed to fight back to the surface, but she was still dizzy and fighting for consciousness. Through water-logged eyes she glimpsed Renato speeding away from her, unaware that she'd vanished. She screamed after him, knowing he couldn't hear her. Then she was sinking again, into deep, deadly water, and despair.

She fought back up again, but she knew she could drown before he even knew that she'd gone. When he returned it would be too late. She felt her consciousness start to fade as weights dragged her down for the last time, and the world grew darker....

The arms that seized her seemed to come from no-where. She could see nothing, but she could feel herself being forced upwards. There was light above, air, gasping relief. She had her arms about Renato's neck, clinging to him.

'I looked back and you were gone,' he said, his voice hoarse with fear. 'What happened—?'

'I don't know—I can't—'

'Never mind. Thank God you're safe.'

The jet ski was a little way off, having stopped when he dived into the water for her. Now he swam over, using his one free arm, and clambered aboard, keeping firm hold of her with one hand. Then he hauled her up in front. 'I want you where I can see you,' he growled. 'You vanished beneath the water—*and I didn't know where to look.*'

His horror matched her own. She clung to him, trembling violently. 'I thought nobody would ever find me,' she gasped.

'It's all right, hold onto to me. Hold on tightly to—' a shudder racked him '—*to your brother.*'

He made a moderate pace back to the ship, with Heather sitting sideways, clinging onto him. She was beyond thought. She just didn't want to let him go. Her consciousness was coming and going in waves. At last she felt herself being hauled aboard, then Renato lifting her and carrying her below to her cabin, then darkness.

When she awoke, Angie was there with her.

'Hello,' her friend said, smiling. 'Surprised to see me? Renato called Bernardo on his mobile, and asked him to bring me to the harbour. I came on board a couple of minutes ago. Trust you to get in the wars.'

Heather was recovered enough to say wickedly, 'I hope you weren't interrupted at too difficult a moment.'

Angie's smile was both impish and mysterious. 'There'll be others. Let me help you get dressed and we'll go ashore.'

'I'll just put something over my swimsuit—'

'What swimsuit?'

Then Heather realised that she was wearing a towelling robe and nothing else. She tried to remember taking off her bathing costume, but her last memory was of Renato laying her down on the bed and kicking the door shut.

'Did you—?'

'Not me,' Angie said. 'You were like that when I got here.' Her face was demure but her eyes were mischievous. 'It's all right. I won't tell Lorenzo.'

'Don't be ridiculous,' Heather said hastily, feeling a blush start in her face and spread all over her body. 'Let's just go home.'

On Angie's orders Heather spent the next day in bed. She slept like a log and awoke feeling good. But when Baptista or Angie dropped in, she thought she sensed a certain tension that they wouldn't talk about. She couldn't ask Renato, because he didn't come to see her at all.

At last Angie explained. 'Renato called Lorenzo in Stockholm to tell him to come home, but he'd never checked into his hotel and nobody knew where he was. So everyone got a little uptight. But it turned out that he was already heading this way.'

'He was coming home anyway?' Heather asked.

'I guess he couldn't bear being away from you. He'll be here later today.'

The knowledge galvanised her to get up, and by afternoon she was looking her best for Lorenzo. As soon as the car stopped he hurried up the steps to clasp her in his arms. He seemed tense and distraught, but she put that down to concern for her safety, and when he said, 'Where's Renato? I have to talk to him, *now*,' she guessed he was going to berate him for allowing her into danger.

'Darling, I'm all right,' she said.

'We'll talk later,' he told her. 'Later. *Renato*.'

He vanished into the house and she didn't see him again that day. Angie and Baptista made her go to bed early, and when she awoke next day the sun was up and Lorenzo was waiting for her at breakfast. He was pale but composed, and he smiled as he promised her he hadn't quarrelled with his brother.

They saw little of each other after that. Renato didn't send him abroad again, but kept him at Head Office in Palermo. Each morning the two of them would leave early for work, and return late.

Heather had no time to miss him. She was enjoying her flowering relationship with Baptista. The old woman showed her all over the house, and she began to understand a little better the family into which she was marrying. Renato had said, 'If you marry one Martelli, you get the whole pack of us,' and it was true.

Looking through photograph albums, she saw the wedding pictures of the young Baptista and Vincente Martelli, the extravagantly beautiful bride barely coming up to the shoulder of her unsmiling groom. He looked several years older, and stood straight and uncomfortable. His face was uncannily like that of Renato today.

Then the early pictures of Renato himself, always looking straight into camera, his dark eyes full of challenge, his mouth uncompromising. Right from the first this had been a young man who knew who he was, what he wanted, and how he was going to get it.

Then Lorenzo appeared, curly-haired, angelic, bringing forth Heather's answering smile. At last there was Bernardo, grave-faced, always standing a little apart, looking as though he wanted to be anywhere else.

'And soon there will be more photographs,' Baptista said, 'when we welcome you into the family.'

Baptista suffered from a weak heart, and spent much of her time resting, but one morning she appeared at breakfast looking strong and cheerful, and invited Heather to take a short trip with her, although wouldn't say where they were going.

'I would have invited Angie as well,' she said as the car took them inland, 'but she and Bernardo had already made plans.' She gave a conspiratorial smile.

'I've never seen Angie like this before,' Heather admitted. 'Usually she's a bit—well—'

'Love 'em and leave 'em,' said Baptista robustly. She was proud of her grasp of English idiom.

'Yes, but she seems really absorbed in Bernardo. I wonder about him, though.'

'He's a very difficult man, but since Angie has been here I've seen him happier than ever before. She may have more to contend with than she imagines, but it will be so nice for all of us if it works out.'

Inland Sicily was more sparsely populated than the coast. Now they were in the rural heartland, where goats grazed within sight of the ruins of a Greek temple. Their way was briefly barred by a flock of sheep, driven by a little nut-brown man with a gap-toothed grin. He nudged his flock to the side and hailed Baptista, who hailed him back.

'We're on my land now,' she explained. 'I have a small estate, a village, some olive groves, and a little villa. It was my dowry.'

At last they saw the village, called Ellona, clinging to the side of the hill. It was a medieval place with cobblestones, tiny houses and only two buildings of note. One was the church, and the other a pink stone villa with two staircases curving up the outside.

The midday heat was at its height, and they sat just inside the house, at a French door looking out onto a terrace, with the net curtains moving gently in the faint breeze.

'I ordered English tea in your honour,' Baptista said, with a note of triumph.

'It's delicious,' Heather said, sipping the Earl Grey. '*Deliziusu.*' She pronounced the Sicilian word very deliberately, to differentiate it from the Italian, *delicioso*. Baptista smiled.

'Already you are becoming a Sicilian,' she said.

'Well, I learned some Italian to get on in the store, and Sicilian isn't too hard if you remember how often it uses "u" where Italian uses "o". I'll get the hang of it.'

'What matters is that you are working hard to become one of us, just as I knew you would.'

'I'll tell you something,' Heather said impulsively. 'I've only been in Sicily a few days, but as soon as I arrived I had such a feeling of—of *rightness*. I don't know how else to say it, but it's as though everything was conspiring to tell me that this is where I belong. I've never had that sense before.'

'Then you have come to the right place, and the right people.' Baptista made a sweep of her hand, indicating the sunlit landscape, down the valley, across to Palermo, with a faint glimpse of the sea beyond. 'See, the very land welcomes you.'

'This place is so beautiful. Did you live here when you were a child?'

'No, but we visited sometimes in the summer, when the city was too hot. It was my property, to be kept in good condition so that it could be a fine dowry when my marriage was arranged.'

'Arranged?' Heather echoed, not sure she'd heard correctly. 'An *arranged* marriage?'

Baptista chuckled. 'Of course. Arranged marriages were very common, and even today—where there is property—' she gave an eloquent shrug. 'They often work out very well, despite what you think.'

'But what about love?'

A faraway look came into Baptista's eyes. 'I was in love once,' she said softly. 'His name was Federico. I called him Fede. He was a fine-looking boy, tall and strong with dark, speaking eyes, and hands that could hold a woman so gently.'

She smiled, looking at something deep inside herself. 'Of course, a well brought up young girl wasn't supposed to notice things like that, but he was the most handsome young man in Sicily. All the girls were crazy for him, but I was the one he loved.'

'What happened?' Heather asked.

'Oh, we never had a chance. He was a gardener, and in those days rich girls didn't marry gardeners. In fact they still don't. He used to work here and grow such beautiful roses, just for me. He said that whenever he saw a rose, he thought of me.'

'What happened?'

'My parents separated us. He was sent away and I never saw or heard of him again. I tried to find out what had become of him, for I thought if only I could know that he was well I might find a sort of peace. But I never managed to discover anything. He had vanished into a void. That was the hardest thing of all to bear.'

'Vanished?' Heather echoed, shocked. 'Do you mean that—?'

'I don't know,' Baptista said quickly. 'He vanished. It would be nice to know, one way or the other, but I suppose now I never will.'

'You still think of him—after all these years?'

'He was my one true love, and no woman ever forgets the man who is that,' Baptista murmured with a touch of wistfulness. 'I cried for weeks, and was sure my life was over. My parents arranged marriages for me and I refused them all. After several years they were growing worried. I was already twenty-five, a late age for a girl of my generation to marry. Finally they suggested Vincente. He was a good man, although very dull. But I wanted children. So I married him, and I was glad.'

'You fell in love?'

'No, not I with him, nor he with me. But we became dear friends.' She gave Heather an impish smile. 'How easy it is to embarrass the young. You are wondering if I knew about my husband and Bernardo's mother. Of course I did, and it wasn't the end of the world. I'd had my love, and the happiness I knew in that short time will stay with me all my days. I was glad Vincente could also be happy.'

'But are you saying that—that love doesn't matter in marriage?'

'I'm saying there is more than one kind of love. Vincente was my dearest friend. As friends we loved each other, and our marriage was strong. When our little girl died we wept in each other's arms.'

'You had a daughter?'

'Our first child. She died when she was six months old. Her name was Doretta.' Baptista took her hand. 'If she had lived, I hope she would have grown up like you, gentle, sweet-natured and strong.'

Heather laid her other hand over Baptista's and looked at her with eyes that were suddenly blurred.

'We haven't known each other very long,' Baptista said, 'but sometimes a few days is enough—as you and Lorenzo have discovered. I knew from the first that you were the daughter of my heart, as surely as if I'd given birth to you. Bella Rosaria would have been Doretta's dowry. Now it will be yours.'

'You mean—you're giving it to Lorenzo—?'

'No. I am giving it to you.'

'But—I couldn't possibly—'

'If you refuse, you will break my heart,' Baptista said simply.

'And I wouldn't hurt you for the world,' Heather said at once. 'Thank you.'

After all, she thought, the property would return to the family on her wedding day. And that was so close now that the gift probably wouldn't happen until the actual wedding.

But Baptista had another surprise for her. She rapped on the floor with her walking stick, and when a maid looked in spoke a few words in Sicilian. A moment later two grave-looking men, dressed in black, entered the room, carrying papers.

'This is my lawyer and his assistant,' Baptista explained. 'The papers are all ready for signature, and they will act as witnesses.'

'You mean now?' Heather asked, slightly aghast.

'There will never be a better time,' Baptista said calmly taking up a pen.

'*Signora*—' Heather said urgently.

'In a few days it will be right for you to call me Mamma,' Baptista observed. 'Why not now? It would make me so happy.'

'And me—Mamma.'

'*Bene!* Now be a dutiful daughter and don't argue.'

A few moments later Heather found herself the owner of an estate. They all marked the occasion with a glass of Marsala, and the lawyers departed.

'Now I'm feeling a little tired,' Baptista announced. 'I'll go and lie down for a while, and you can look over your property.'

As she wandered through the rooms of the elegant little villa Heather knew she'd found the true home she wanted. It was the perfect size for two people in love, and just close enough to Palermo to make it feasible for her and Lorenzo to live here.

Plans were forming in her mind. Since she could travel with him it would be easy for her to involve herself in his work. Baptista had a seat on the board, and was all for Heather taking an interest in the firm. She and Lorenzo could work together and then retreat to this magic place and make their own world.

And when their world began to grow she knew exactly the room she wanted for a nursery. It was at the back of the house, overlooking the magnificent, flower-filled gardens. She stood at the window a moment, mentally re-decorating this room in pastel shades, then hurried down to explore the grounds.

Here the air was heady with a thousand scents. Tall trees shaded her progress and birds called overhead as she wandered in a place of pure enchantment. Always she was within sound of rushing water, and sometimes she came upon little fountains, cut into the walls.

Suddenly the path widened into a small arbour, almost separate from the rest of the garden. Everywhere she looked there were roses, pink, white, yellow, climbing roses, trailing roses, full blooms and small tight buds. And in the centre a bush of brilliant crimson blooms that was in itself a declaration of love.

'I thought you would find this place,' Baptista said.

Heather turned and saw her standing there, leaning slightly on her stick.

'I saw you from my window, and wanted to show you my special place myself.'

'Did he—?'

'Yes, Fede began it for me. It was his way of saying what he dared not say in words.'

She indicated a small wooden bench and they sat there together.

'Over the years I have tended this place with love and it has grown. I've protected the plants so that they survived the winters, taking them into greenhouses, or even the house. Some are still the original plants that he put here. Some are from cuttings.

'And I have taken cuttings to the Residenza, and put them in my garden there. But here, in this spot, was where he said to me that no other woman would ever exist for him besides me.'

She pointed to the glorious red blooms. 'We planted

that together, and I have never let it die,' she said softly. 'If he came back now, I could show him that bush and say, "See how I have loved it for your sake."'

'And I shall love it for yours,' Heather said softly.

'I knew you would. And when they bury me, and my coffin is piled high with formal tributes from people I cared nothing about, will you make sure a single bloom from this bush lies hidden there somewhere?'

'Of course I will. But don't you want Lorenzo or Renato to do that for you?'

She shook her head. 'When the time comes Lorenzo will sob and forget everything but his grief. You will have to be strong for him then. And Renato is a good man, but there are things about the heart that he doesn't understand.'

'Just about everything, I should think,' Heather said, and the two women exchanged a smile. 'Of course I'll do this for you,' she promised.

'Then I can be peaceful, for it was troubling me that there was nobody I could rely on to do this.'

'You still love him, after so long?'

'Not as I think you mean it. Passion is long dead. What matters then is someone to sit with you in the evening sun: someone who will talk and hold your hand, and smile at you with eyes that say, "Let us go, unafraid, into the twilight together." Sometimes at dusk I'll come and sit here, and remember. But always I sit alone. I am growing old, my dear daughter, and my heart aches for what I shall never have.'

She tucked her hand in Heather's arm, and slowly they made their way back to the house.

Lorenzo's reaction later that night was strange. After the first surprise and pleasure, he said, 'I wonder how

Renato will take this. He always hoped to own Bella Rosaria one day.'

After which Heather braced herself for recriminations, but Renato went up to his room without giving her more than a brief nod.

Renato will take this. He always longed to own Bella Rosaria too.

After which it later traced through the recriminations but Renato went on refusing, and about giving Lorenzo him a final nod.

CHAPTER FIVE

RELATIVES were beginning to converge on Palermo, some to stay in the Residenza, others to occupy the biggest suites in the best hotels. Heather was astonished by the legions of aunts, uncles, cousins that made up the far reaching branches of the Martelli family.

She met people until she was giddy. The ones she enjoyed the most were Enrico and Giuseppe. They were first cousins to each other, and distant cousins to Baptista, and long ago they had both been in love with her. When she married Vincente Martelli, they had consoled each other's broken hearts. Forty years later they were still bachelors, still competing for the honour of escorting her. She was allowing them both to squire her to the wedding. Otherwise there would have been a riot.

Two days before the wedding the great house was gleaming in readiness for the wedding ball. In their bedroom upstairs, Angie and Heather prepared for an evening of dancing.

After her day on the boat Heather had tanned to a pale biscuit colour that was very becoming. It was a pity, she thought, as she stepped out of the shower, that she couldn't be the same perfect colour all over. But that would have meant sunbathing naked...

Suddenly she could feel Renato's hands gliding over her shoulders and down her spine, lulling her into a warm, hypnotic daze that made everything else unimportant. And later he'd stripped her naked in the cabin. She pressed her hands against her cheeks, which were suddenly burning, wishing desperately that these strange fancies would cease tormenting her.

'Hurry up!' Angie called.

'Coming,' she said with relief.

Lorenzo kissed her hand when he saw her in pale lavender embroidered silk. 'Every man there will envy me,' he declared. Despite his gallant words his air was abstracted. But they were all under a strain, she thought.

There was a burst of applause as they opened the ball together, making the first circuit of the floor alone before the others joined them. Heather had the feeling that everything was happening in slow motion, so that as she whirled in Lorenzo's arms she had time to see the faces watching them. There was Baptista, flanked by her two cavaliers, smiling contentedly as she saw her dream come true. There were Angie and Bernardo, already looking like a settled couple. Everything was wonderful.

Then she noticed Renato standing close to the most extravagantly lovely woman she had ever seen. She was a ripe brunette in the full summer of her beauty. Her mouth was ripe and luscious, her dark eyes were as huge and vacant as a cow's. Everything about her proclaimed lasciviousness, including the speaking look she was directing up at Renato.

'Careful,' Lorenzo said, tightening his grip on her. 'You nearly stumbled.'

'Sorry,' she said breathlessly.

'You were miles away. What were you thinking of?'

'Why—our wedding, of course,' she said with a bright laugh. 'I think of it all the time.'

'So do I—the day after tomorrow—and then we'll tie the knot for ever.'

'Yes—for ever.'

'Thank goodness the others are starting to dance. I don't feel so conspicuous.'

'Who's that woman with Renato?'

'That's Elena Alante, she's a widow. Renato prefers them married, divorced or widowed. Experienced, anyway. The one over there is Minetta, and just behind her is the Contessa Julia Bennotti. All three of them are—well, Renato is—'

'A brave man,' Heather suggested lightly.

'Very brave to have them all here at once. I wonder what possessed him.'

Heather wondered too when she finally came face to face with Renato. He looked more tense and edgy than she'd seen him before, like a man with a fiend sitting on his shoulder. He greeted Heather with a nod and a smile that seemed to take a lot of effort, and introduced her to Elena. As the two women inclined their heads in greeting Heather became aware of something that made her smile.

'Allow me to congratulate you on your perfume, *signora*,' she murmured. 'It's delightful.'

'Dear Renato bought it for me recently,' Elena cooed. 'It's called "Deep In The Night". I keep telling him he shouldn't buy me so many expensive gifts, but he says I'm special to him.'

'And for a special friend a man buys a special gift,' Heather murmured. 'I'm sure he took a lot of trouble to choose exactly the right perfume for you.'

'I think it's time I had the privilege of dancing with the bride,' Renato said curtly, taking her hand. Heather let him lead her onto the floor, where another waltz was just beginning.

'That's enough of your tricks,' he growled.

'I was only being polite. It really is a lovely perfume.

And since you had the nerve to flaunt your harem, surely you shouldn't be shy about them?'

'There are some things best not talked about,' he growled, a warning light in his eyes.

'Not a guilty conscience, surely?'

'No, just a sense of propriety,' he snapped.

A bitter demon drove her to say, 'Propriety? You? I wish I'd been a fly on the wall when you gave Elena that perfume, with a gallant speech about how she haunted your thoughts while you were in London—that is, the thoughts you could spare from Julia and Minetta, and, of course, when you weren't propositioning your brother's girlfriend—'

His hand in the small of her back tightened. 'Stop it,' he whispered. 'Don't dare to talk like that.'

'I—' It was suddenly hard to breathe. 'I was only making small talk.' She pulled herself together. 'I haven't yet thanked you for a delightful day out. You were right about spending our honeymoon on your boat.' She was spinning words, any words, barely knowing what she said.

'One thing I wasn't right about,' he grated. 'You and Lorenzo must find somewhere else to live.'

'But you said—'

'I've changed my mind. *You can't live here.*'

No need to ask why. She'd been wrong about the fiend. It wasn't on his shoulder, but in his heart. It looked out from his eyes and told her that he was on hot coals. Just as she was.

She became aware that he was breathing harshly. She tried to tell herself that it was merely the exertion of dancing, but the truth was there between them. If they had been alone he would have kissed her. And then he would have kissed her again, long, hard and passionately. And she would have kissed him back in the way they'd both foreseen on that long ago day when he'd come to her counter and the air had been jagged between them from the first moment.

It was all wrong. She loved Lorenzo dearly, so how could she be on fire at the thought of laying her lips against Renato's and feeling his arms about her? How could it be his body she ached to feel pressed against hers, his hands on her skin with the purposeful yet sensitive touch she'd felt once before? It had haunted her every moment since. She could admit that now.

It would have been easier if she'd stayed hostile to him, but their moment of sympathy on the beach had destroyed that. She'd discovered that she could like him, even be sad for him. That was even more dangerous than her body's wayward reaction.

'I shouldn't dance with you,' she blurted out in sudden dread.

'I know,' he said quietly.

'I meant—I have so many duty dances to do. I shouldn't waste one with *miu frati*.'

But the words were a mistake. They recalled the picnic when he'd spoken to her with a quiet intensity she suddenly didn't want to remember.

'You're right,' he said. 'You must return to your duty, and I must return to my "harem". They suit me. They cause me no problems.'

'I'm sure nobody could cause you a problem that you couldn't solve, Renato.'

'Once I thought so too. The dance is ending. Goodnight—until I lead you to the altar to marry my brother.'

She turned away to meet one of the many Martelli relations who mustn't be overlooked. After him there was another, and so her whole evening was taken up, and she didn't have to look at Renato, or wonder who he was dancing with.

The world was shrouded in mist. Through it she was vaguely aware of strong arms carrying her down steps, laying her on a bed, hands moving over her bikini, stripping it from her body. She felt the slight breeze on her naked flesh, a towel dabbing her dry, her breasts, her thighs—

And then, piercing the mist, the man's face, his eyes defenceless, appalled at his own thoughts.

Suddenly it all vanished, and Heather found she was sitting up in bed, shuddering, her body alive with unwanted sensation. 'No,' she gasped. *'No!'*

'What is it?' Angie asked, scrambling out of her own bed and hurrying to her. 'Heather, what's the matter?'

'Nothing—just a dream—'

Just a dream in which the memory she'd fiercely suppressed had forced its way into view. She hadn't dared remember how she'd lain naked in Renato's arms, or how he'd looked at her. But part of her would never forget.

'I'm going for a walk,' she said.

'Shall I come with you?'

'No, thank you. I—I need to be alone.'

Throwing a light robe over her nightdress, she slipped out onto the terrace. The house was quiet and dark, and here in the cool night air she might soothe the fever that consumed her. It was two in the morning. Her wedding day. And she had been wrenched awake by a dream of another man.

In her heart she'd always known Renato was dangerous. But it would pass once she was married. In Lorenzo's arms, in his bed, she would forget everything else. She *must!*

She looked over the terrace rail to the one below and what she saw filled her with relief. 'Lorenzo,' she called in a whisper. 'I'm coming down.'

She returned through her room and slipped out, along the corridor, down the stairs. He was waiting for her in the hall, his arms open to receive her as she flung herself against him.

'What is it, darling? What's wrong?'

'Nothing. I just wanted to say how much I love you—love you—*love you*—'

'There's no need to sound so upset about it.'

'I'm not upset. Everything's perfect. But I had to tell you that I love you.'

'And I love you, so everything's all right.'

He kissed her. Heather gave herself up to that kiss, trying to find in it everything she wanted. But no kiss could give that. They were both too full of tension. Things would be different when they were on the boat, drifting beneath the moonlight.

She jumped at a sudden sound from the darkness. 'What was that?'

'Only Renato. That's his study. He's actually in there, working.'

'Could he have heard us?'

'Probably. What does it matter? Forget him. Why, darling, you're trembling.' Lorenzo's arms went around her. 'Let me take you upstairs. Just a few more hours, and we'll belong to each other for ever.'

The wedding dress was made of silk-satin, designed in a subtly medieval style, with the skirt falling in heavy folds from her waist, and the slight fullness coming from the huge amount of material that had been used. At the back it stretched out into a long train embellished around the hem with French lace. The sleeves were plain to the elbows, then flared into more lace. The veil stretched almost down to the floor, held in place by the pearl tiara. The effect of it with the dress was elegant and breathtaking.

The sensation of becoming a new person, that had come upon her gradually since she'd been here, was stronger now. Her day on the boat had bleached her light brown hair to gold; her lightly tanned skin made the whites of her eyes glow with brilliant effect. For the first time in her life she was not merely pretty but beautiful, even glamorous.

The heat of Sicily had done this to her, as it had also warmed her body, awakening her to physical sensations that had lain dormant in the mists of England. It was the heat of the furnace, and some northerners wilted in it. But Heather had flowered.

As bridesmaid, Angie wore a simple cream silk that brought out the glow of her skin and her dark eyes, full of pleasurable anticipation. Heather smiled at her.

'I believe some Sicilian wedding customs are the same as those in England,' she teased. 'Like the one about the bridesmaid and the best man.' Bernardo was the best man.

There was a knock on the door, and Renato called. 'Everyone has gone to the cathedral. Bernardo and Lorenzo left several minutes ago. I'm waiting for you downstairs.'

Angie presented Heather with her bouquet of white roses. 'You look fantastic. Lorenzo will keel over when he sees you.'

Heather smiled. In the bright sunlight her troubling fancies had faded. She loved Lorenzo and he loved her. That was all that mattered.

They made a slow procession along the corridor, then a slight turn so that Heather was looking down the broad staircase. Every servant in the house seemed to be gathered there to see her entrance, all beaming up at her with approval. And there was Renato, gazing up as the bride began her stately descent. His face bore a rigid look, as though he was holding his breath. Then he stepped forward, extending his hand. She placed her own hand in it, and he steadied her down the last few steps, while the servants applauded.

The limousine was waiting. Heather climbed carefully into the back and sat while Angie settled her dress and veil perfectly about her, then got in beside her. Renato joined them, and they were ready to go.

At first she looked out of the window at the scenery as they glided slowly down towards Palermo, trying to take in that this was really happening to her. Renato was silent, and she thought he too must be preoccupied, but when she turned to him she found his gaze fixed on her. In his eyes was the same stunned look she'd seen earlier.

They had reached the outskirts of Palermo and the car was making its way through the streets until at last the great cathedral was in sight. Both cars were drawing to a halt, the doors were opening.

She stood in the bright sunlight while Angie straightened her dress, then fell into place behind her. There was a little crowd nearby. They stopped to look at the wedding party. Some of them applauded, and Heather heard the whisper, *'Grazziusu.'* Beautiful.

Renato looked at her.

'Are you ready?'

'Quite ready.'

'No doubts?'

'Why do you ask that?' she cried.

'I don't know,' he said abruptly. 'Let's go.'

She took the arm he offered, and they walked across the piazza and into the cathedral together.

After the brilliance outside the dim light was like darkness, but then her eyes focused on the magnificent interior full of guests, all turning to watch her arrive. Beyond them she could see the choir, and the archbishop waiting by the altar to marry her to Lorenzo.

High overhead the organ pealed out. She took a deep breath, her hand tightened unconsciously on Renato's arm, and she prepared for the first step.

'Wait,' Renato said softly.

Then she saw Bernardo hurrying down the aisle towards them. He looked worried. 'Not yet,' he said in a low, urgent voice. 'Lorenzo isn't here.'

'What do you mean?' Renato demanded. 'You arrived together, didn't you?'

'Yes, but then he slipped away. He said he needed to have a word with someone, and he'd be back in a moment but when I went to look for him, nobody knew where he was, and—'

'And what?' Renato asked harshly, for Bernardo seemed unwilling to continue.

'I spoke to a woman outside. She'd seen a young man get into a taxi. From the description—but it might have been anyone, of course—'

'Of course it might,' Renato broke in. 'A storm in a teacup. Lorenzo will return in a minute.'

But behind the apparent conviction Heather heard the uneasy note in his voice, and she saw that Bernardo couldn't meet her eye.

Even so, it wasn't real. She felt as though she were floating in a place where there was no sensation, and from where she could look down on a woman in a bridal gown, staring disaster in the face. It was somebody else.

'What has happened? Where is Lorenzo?'

Nobody had seen Baptista approach down the aisle. Now she was there, a tiny, commanding figure, clinging to Enrico's arm, looking from one to the other. 'Where is Lorenzo?' she repeated.

For a ghastly moment nobody knew how to answer her. Then there was a small commotion outside, and a boy of about sixteen hurried in and came to a nervous halt at the sight of the group. He gulped, thrust a sheet of paper into the bridal bouquet, and ran for his life.

She was floating again, watching the bride carefully remove the paper and hand the beautiful flowers to the bridesmaid. There wasn't even an envelope, just something in pencil on a sheet. It was scrawled, as though it had been written in a hurry, or great agitation, or both.

Dearest, darling Heather,

Please forgive me. I wouldn't have done it like this if there had been any other way, but Renato was so set on this marriage that I haven't known whether I was coming or going.

I do love you—I think. And maybe if things had happened naturally between us we would have married anyway, in time. We had a lovely romance, didn't we? If only it could have stayed that way. But Renato descended on us in London. It suited him for us to marry, and you know the rest.

And then he was injured and you saved him. You looked so marvellous to me that night that marriage didn't seem so bad any more. And suddenly everything was arranged and I was practically an old married man before I'd had time to enjoy being young.

I came back from Stockholm early to talk to you,

explain why we ought to postpone everything for a while, but Renato made me 'see reason' (his words).

So I suppose when I set out this morning I really meant to go through with it. But when I was sitting in the cathedral I suddenly knew I couldn't.

Try to forgive me. I still think you're wonderful.

Lorenzo.

The silence seemed to be singing in Heather's ears, but it was a strange kind of silence that sounded almost like laughing. The whole world was laughing. Slowly she lowered the sheet of paper, staring into space.

Lorenzo wasn't coming. He'd never loved her very much, never truly wanted to marry her at all. Renato had wanted their marriage, 'because it suited him.' For his own convenience he'd moved them around like puppets, pulling strings here, bending the truth a little there. No wonder he'd welcomed her so enthusiastically.

Behind her she heard Renato's furious Sicilian curse, *'Malediri!'* and understood that he'd read the letter over her shoulder. As if drawn by a magnet she turned to look at him and saw his eyes full of shock. It had drained the colour from beneath his tan, so that he looked almost the same as in the ambulance, the night he'd nearly died.

He met her gaze. For once he wasn't in command. He looked as she felt, like someone who'd received a savage blow in the stomach. Later Heather was to remember that, but now it made little impact. She still had the sense of floating above everything.

Curious relatives had started to drift up the aisle to get a better look. More and more of them came as the news whispered through the congregation that something had gone horribly, excitingly wrong.

'What does he say?' Angie whispered.

Receiving no answer, she took the page from Heather's nerveless fingers. Bernardo too contrived to read it, then raised his head to meet Renato's eyes, his own angry and astonished. 'I'll find him, bring him back—'

'No!' Heather said violently. Her head cleared and she looked round at them. 'Do you think I'd marry him now?'

'Heather, he doesn't really mean it,' Bernardo pleaded.

'*I* mean it. Do you think I'm so desperate for a wedding ring that I'll marry a man at gunpoint? How dare you!'

He nodded. 'Forgive me! It was a foolish thing to say.'

Her strength was coming back. Inwardly she was screaming, and some time very soon there would be bitter tears. But right now she seemed to be made of pure pride, and it would sustain her until she was alone. If only she could run away now, and hide from the crowd who'd witnessed her humiliation. But she wouldn't run. She wouldn't hide. She would face them with her head up.

'Right,' she said calmly. 'That's that, then. We'd better go home.' She looked Renato in the eye. 'You brought me. You can take me back.'

There was a look of pure admiration in his eyes, if she hadn't been too angry to see it. But her anger faded as she looked at Baptista, who had been standing there in silence. The old woman looked wretchedly ill and frail.

'I'm sorry, Mamma. This is terrible for you too.'

Baptista managed a tired smile. 'Try to forgive my son, if you can. He means well, but he always did what was easiest. I spoiled and indulged him, and this is the result.'

'None of this is your fault,' Heather said emphatically. She looked directly at Renato, but didn't underline the look with words.

'You're very kind, my dear,' Baptista said faintly. 'Very kind—' she swayed and her eyes closed.

'Mamma!' Renato said sharply, and put his arms out just in time.

'Lay her down,' Angie said, turning in a moment from a bridesmaid into a doctor. She knelt beside Baptista, felt her heart, frowning.

'Is it a heart attack?' Renato asked tensely, kneeling on the other side.

'I'm not sure. It may not be too serious, but she needs to get to the hospital.'

Renato raised his mother in his arms. 'Mamma,' he said urgently. 'Mamma! *Miu Diu!*' Still carrying her, he strode to the door. 'The hospital is close. We'll go straight there.'

'Leave the guests to us,' Enrico said. 'We'll take them home, see they're fed, and get rid of them.'

'Thank you,' Bernardo said fervently, following his brother.

'What do we do?' Angie asked Heather.

'We follow,' Heather said firmly. 'I love her too.'

Outside they commandeered one of the wedding cars and directed the driver. They reached the hospital to find Bernardo and Renato in the corridor, pacing about.

'Is there any news?' Heather asked, not looking at Renato. She wanted to pretend that he didn't exist. Her mind was so full of misery and turmoil that it was only by concentrating on Baptista that she could keep from screaming.

'Not yet, but I'm sure she'll be all right,' Bernardo said. 'She's had giddy spells before, and always recovered.'

'But each one brings her closer to the end,' Renato said wretchedly. 'Her heart could give out at any time; we've always known that.'

'I think you're being too gloomy,' Angie said firmly. 'It didn't look like a heart attack to me. Just a faint. And I am a doctor, don't forget.'

Bernardo threw her a grateful look, and Heather didn't miss the way he squeezed Angie's hand, or the reassuring smiles they exchanged. How right they seemed together: as perfect for each other as she had once thought she and Lorenzo—

A shuddering gasp broke from her, and for a moment her eyes filled with tears. Through the blur she could see the magnificence of her dress swirling around her. At this moment she should be kneeling before the altar at Lorenzo's side, while the priest intoned the words that made them each other's for ever. Instead it had all been a mockery. And the man who'd schemed and manipulated to bring this disaster down on all their heads was Renato.

Heather had never hated any human being before in her life, but at this moment the taste of hatred was bitter in her mouth. She looked up to find Renato watching her, and knew that he'd read her thoughts. She wanted to hurl bitter accusations at his head, but the sight of his ravaged face stopped her. Angrily she brushed the tears away from her eyes. His mother was ill. She wouldn't curse him, but neither would she let him see her weeping, or showing any sign of weakness.

'Darling,' Angie whispered, reaching out to her.

'I'm all right,' Heather said firmly, pulling herself together. 'Bernardo, I should like to ask you a favour.'

'Of course,' he said at once.

'Would you telephone home, please, and speak to Baptista's maid? Ask her to bring me some day clothes to change into.'

'And me,' Angie said quickly.

He nodded and moved away to a quiet corner, taking out his mobile. Heather went to the window and stood looking out. If she didn't have to look at Renato she might just about endure this.

Bernardo returned to say the maid was on her way, just as a doctor appeared.

'She's stable,' he said. 'You can see her just for a moment.'

The two men departed. Angie and Heather sat in silence until the clothes arrived. Within a few minutes they were plainly dressed, and nobody could have told that there was ever going to be a wedding.

Renato emerged into the corridor. Beneath his tan his face had a kind of greyish pallor and his voice sounded strained. 'My mother would like to see you,' he told Heather.

'How is she?'

'Suffering terribly. She blames herself for this disaster.'

'That's nonsense. I know who's to blame and it isn't her.'

'Then tell her that. Tell her anything you like, but for God's sake stop her torturing herself. You're the only one who can help her now.'

Heather slipped past him into Baptista's room. Bernardo rose from the bed and backed away as she approached. Renato came just inside the room and stood there, watching as Heather approached the bed.

Only a short time ago the old woman had looked magnificent and indomitable in black satin, lace and diamonds. Now she looked frail and tiny, lying against the white sheets, her face drained of colour. She turned her head towards Heather. Her eyes were tired and anxious.

'Forgive me,' she whispered. 'Forgive me...'

'There's nothing to forgive,' Heather said quickly. 'This isn't your fault.'

'My son—has dishonoured you—'

'No,' Heather said firmly. 'I can only be dishonoured by my own actions. Not somebody else's. There is no dishonour. This will pass, and life will go on.' She took Baptista's hand. 'For you too.'

Baptista searched her face. 'I think you have—a great heart—' she murmured. 'My son is a fool.'

Heather leaned closer, smiling into the old woman's eyes, trying to reassure her. 'Most men are fools,' she said. 'We know that, don't we? But we don't have to be affected by their foolishness.'

Baptista's face relaxed, and she seemed drawn into the kindly female conspiracy Heather was offering her. 'Bless you,' she whispered. 'Don't go.'

'Not just yet,' Heather agreed. 'Not until I know you're on the mend.'

'I'll be home soon. Promise me that I'll find you there.' Baptista's voice grew urgent. 'Promise me.'

Heather stared at her in dismay. All she wanted was to flee Sicily.

'Please—' she started to say, 'I can't—'

'Promise her!' Renato said violently.

Baptista was growing dangerously agitated. Heather spoke quickly. 'I promise,' she said. 'I'll be there when you come home. But I'll go now so that you can be alone with your family.'

'You will be there,' Baptista repeated. 'You have given your word.'

'And I'm a woman of my word. Don't worry.' She slipped out.

'What is it?' Angie asked quickly, seeing her pale face.

'I can't believe what I've done.' Briefly she told Angie what had happened.

'You didn't have any choice.'

'No, I didn't. But how do I live in the same house with Renato without telling him how much I hate him?'

CHAPTER SIX

THE Residenza was eerily quiet. The vast hordes of guests had swarmed all over it, devouring the feast, hungrier and thirstier for the excitement of having something horrifying to talk about. Now they were all gone, save for one or two who lived too far away to depart that night. In the morning they too would vanish.

The wedding cake remained uneaten, because everyone had been too superstitious to touch it. It stood tall and beautiful in its white, shimmering glory, celebrating a lovers' union that would never be.

Heather stood in the semi-darkness of the great hall, looking at the cake, with its tiny bride and groom on the topmost tier. She was trapped in limbo, unable to go forward or back. The way back involved too many painful thoughts. The way forward was blocked by her promise.

She felt slightly giddy, and recalled that she'd eaten nothing since the night before. This morning she'd refused breakfast. Too excited. She would eat later, at the reception, she'd thought. And when they cut the cake she'd planned to take the two little figures from the top and treasure them always. Well, they were still there, if she wanted them.

Suddenly she broke. All day she'd used Baptista's illness to fend off the truth, but now there was nothing to protect her from it. Lorenzo didn't love her, had deserted her in front of the whole cathedral. The dream of love that she'd believed in had turned out to be a monstrous, sickening farce.

At this moment she forgot the doubts that had plagued her only the night before. They belonged in the realm of reason and common sense and it was too soon to heed them.

What tortured her now were memories of the time when Lorenzo had been the young man who charmed her and made life sweet with his kindness, his cheerful good nature, and his adoration. Her feelings for him might have turned out to be no more than infatuation, but they had been real enough in their way, and now they were bitterly painful. She covered her eyes with her hand and leaned forward, swaying against the table, while anguish shook her. Tears threatened but she fought them back.

I will not cry. *I will not cry.*

At least, not now. Not until she could be alone, away from this house, away from this island, away from Renato Martelli.

A footstep made her whirl around. Renato stood there, watching her. Furious at his intrusion, she pulled herself together and spoke as calmly as she could. 'How is your mother?'

'Asleep when I left her. The doctors think it was just a giddy spell.'

'And she's in no danger?'

'She has a bad heart. But this wasn't a heart attack.'

'Fine. Then I can go soon?'

'If you want to hurt her. She has welcomed you as her daughter—'

'But I'm not her daughter,' Heather said harshly, 'nor will I ever be—'

'You don't understand. I'm not talking about legalities. I'm saying that she loves you. From the moment you arrived she opened her arms to you. Didn't you feel that?'

'Yes, I did, and it meant the world to me, but now—'

'Now you'll turn your back on her? Is that how you repay her kindness?'

'I've said I'll stay until she returns home. I can't promise further than that.'

The sound of her own voice startled her. It sounded hard with the effort of suppressing all emotion, not like herself at all. Or perhaps this stern, dry-eyed, controlled woman was who she was now.

One of the family maids was hovering uneasily. She asked Renato something in Sicilian. 'She wants to know what she should do with the cake,' he said.

Heather stared at him, aghast. She was starving, devastated, with every nerve at breaking point, and her exhausted mind on the edge of hallucinating. The prosaic question caught her off guard and almost sent her into hysterics. 'How would I know?' she asked wildly. 'I've never been in this situation before. Oddly enough, the books of wedding etiquette don't cover it. You suggest something. You're the man who has an answer for every problem, *even if some of your answers fall apart at awkward moments.*'

He flinched but stayed calm. 'I'll tell her to send it to the children's home.'

'Good idea. But not the top tier. Ask her to take that down now and give it to me.'

Renato did so. The maid climbed on a chair and reached up to lift down the tiny cake, adorned with the figures under a flowered arch. But her hand shook and the little bridegroom fell to the floor and broke in two. Renato gave her a nod of reassurance, and she hurried away.

'Why do you want that?' he asked as Heather surveyed the small top tier.

'To eat, of course. I think the bride should have some of her own wedding cake, don't you?' She took up a sharp knife and cut into the ornately decorated icing. 'Have some with me.'

'I don't think—'

'Then pour me some champagne. You're not going to deny me wedding cake and champagne on my big day, are you?'

He found two glasses and filled them. 'When did you last eat?'

'Yesterday. I couldn't manage anything this morning.'

'You'll regret drinking champagne on an empty stomach.'

She poured two glasses and thrust one at him. 'Drink it with me. Let's toast the day you brought about.'

'Heather, I know you must hate me—'

'And try contempt and loathing. Especially contempt.'

She drained her champagne glass and refilled it. 'I want to know how much of Lorenzo's letter was true. When he returned from Stockholm early—that was why? To tell you that he wanted to call it all off?'

'Look—'

'Tell me, damn you!'

'Yes,' he said reluctantly. 'He said that.'

'And you kept it to yourself?'

'Why should I tell you what could hurt you? I talked to Lorenzo and—' He seemed to have trouble going on.

'"Made him see reason," was his charming expression. You mean you told him he had to marry me whether he liked it or not. *How dare you?* What do you think I am? Some helpless bird-brain with no guts or independence?'

'No, but after what you told me—about your previous fiancé—'

'You told him *that*?' she cried, aghast. 'Oh, you've done everything you can to humiliate me, haven't you? I can just hear you—"You can't walk out on her, Lorenzo.

The poor creature's already been deserted once. You've got to see it through, however much you'd rather not.''

'Would I have done better to let him walk away from his obligations?'

Eyes flashing, she whirled on him. 'He *did* walk away. You just made sure he did it at the worst possible moment. And why obligations? I was marrying for love and I thought he was doing the same. I don't want a husband who's only doing his duty.

'If we'd broken up in London I could have coped. I'd still have had my job, my friends, my life there. But you wanted our marriage, to suit yourself. You had to play God with people's lives, *to suit yourself*. And now Lorenzo has vanished, I'm stranded and your mother is ill, all because Renato Martelli has to have his own way.'

He didn't answer, but there was a drawn look about his face that checked her. 'I'm sorry,' she said wearily. 'I didn't mean to throw your mother's illness up at you.'

'Why not? It's true.'

'Yes, but I shouldn't have said it. I shouldn't—' Her voice thickened, and she set her jaw. She would not weep. She *would not*.

'Heather—' He reached for her but she backed off, eyes flashing.

'I'm warning you, Renato—if you touch me, there'll be violence.'

He checked himself. 'Perhaps enough has been said for tonight,' he sighed. 'I'm sure you'd prefer me to leave you.'

She didn't answer. Her face was unyielding. As he left her Renato felt a flash of some emotion he could hardly identify. He was a man who feared nothing, so his own dread took him by surprise. He didn't know this woman who looked as though a stone lay where her heart should be. He only knew that he was guilty of some terrible crime.

Next morning, when the last guest had left, Renato sought out Heather and said, 'I thought you should know that I've traced Lorenzo. He's staying with friends in Naples.'

He didn't look directly at her as he spoke. That way he didn't have to notice her pallor, or the signs that she hadn't slept. But he couldn't help knowing that she tensed at the sound of Lorenzo's name.

'Does he know that his mother is ill?' Heather asked quietly.

'No, I haven't spoken to him.'

'You must. He ought to return and see her.'

'There's no need for that,' he said sharply. 'It's not serious. She'll be home tomorrow.'

'But it would mean a lot to her to see him.'

'It might also strain her.'

'I think you're wrong,' Heather said firmly. 'It's much harder for her to wonder about him.'

After a moment's silence she looked up to see Renato regarding her strangely. 'You're very determined to fetch him back,' he said quietly.

Once she'd hardly been aware of having a temper. Now a word from Renato could trigger it. 'If you mean what I think you do, you should be ashamed. It's all over between Lorenzo and me. I'd never marry him now.'

'Perhaps you think you mean that. But if he came back and turned on the charm—'

'Well, you should know all about the power of Lorenzo's charm,' she said bleakly. 'It was you who told him to give me the full blast of it for your own ends.'

She heard the slight intake of his breath and knew she'd

struck home. She was glad, she told herself angrily. Let him suffer as she suffered.

'Besides,' she added, 'he's not very likely to try to win me back, is he? Not after all the trouble he took to escape me.'

Try as she might, she couldn't stop her voice shaking on the last words, and it made Renato say more gently, 'It wasn't you he was escaping, but me. And I know my brother better than you. He values things more when he's lost them.'

She gave him the cool, defiant look that was her way of coping. 'So there's hope yet,' she said ironically. 'Lorenzo will make a play for me, and I'll be fool enough to fall for it. Cue wedding bells, summon all the guests back, and—hey presto! Renato Martelli gets his own way again.'

'*For pity's sake!*' he shouted. 'Can't you understand—?' He checked himself. 'I'm sorry. I just wish I could find the right words to say to you.'

'Does it occur to you that there aren't any?'

'I'm beginning to be afraid that you're right. Heather, won't you let me ask your pardon? I never dreamed of anything like this happening.'

'No, you wanted life arranged your way, and to hell with anyone else. I did a lot of thinking last night, and several things came back to me. Chiefly the fact that nobody mentioned marriage until you did, that night in London. You said Lorenzo was talking about marriage, but that came as news to him. I saw his face. I thought his expression was embarrassment but actually it was surprise.'

'He had told me that if he thought of marriage it would be to you—' Renato said unwillingly.

'*If?* But it was a very big if. I'm almost as angry about

what you've done to Lorenzo as I am about what you've done to me. You pushed him into something he wasn't ready for, and now he's the one who looks bad.'

'He could have stood up to me and refused,' Renato said angrily.

'Oh, please! Who stands up to you?'

'You do.'

'And much good it does me! Now, I think you should get him back here to see his mother. Tell him there'll be no tears or reproaches from me. He's not the one I blame.'

'Not blame him? After what he did to you—?'

'After what *you* did to me. Lorenzo tried to tell me honestly about his doubts, but you stopped him. If he and I could have talked I'd have released him at once, quietly, here at home, instead of having to do it in public. That was your doing, not his. So tell him not to worry.'

After a moment he said, 'If we could talk naturally I could tell you how much I admire you for the dignity and spirit you've shown in this. But I know that my admiration will only provoke your contempt.'

'Right first time,' she said crisply. 'Now, please, go and make that call.'

She spent the day at the hospital. Baptista slept a good deal but when she awoke her eyes sought Heather, always finding her in a chair by the window, and she smiled with relief. When Renato arrived Heather rose to go, but before she could do so she heard him say in a low voice, 'Lorenzo will be home this evening, Mamma.'

She left the room before she could become too aware of them looking at her, and went to have a coffee. Before he left Renato joined her.

'You were right,' he said. 'The news has cheered her

up. It was generous of you to insist. I hope it won't come too hard on you.'

'I have no feelings one way or the other,' she assured him.

'I wish I knew if that were true.'

'Does it matter? It's your mother who counts.'

'But you count too. We need to talk very soon—'

'I don't think so.'

'Surely you can see that matters can't be left like this?'

'Of course. When she's better I'll arrange to return Bella Rosaria, and then I'll go back to England.'

'That wasn't what I meant. There are other things—'

'No, Renato, there's nothing else. I'll go back to her now.

Towards evening Baptista became wakeful, growing alert at every sound.

'He'll be here soon,' Heather promised.

'My dear, will it break your heart to see him?'

'Hearts don't break that easily,' she said with a determined smile.

'I think they do—at least for a while.'

'I'll tell you something,' Heather said in a rush. 'It's not just losing Lorenzo—it's losing everything. That day we went to Bella Rosaria, I told you how right it's all felt since I arrived. I was so sure that fate had brought me to the right place to marry the right man.' She gave an ironic little laugh. 'It just shows you how wrong you can be.'

'I don't think you were wrong,' Baptista said.

'I must have been. I misread every signal, even my own. I'm different. I can't recognise my own reactions. Once this would have made me cry my heart out. Now I just want to do something forceful, to show people that I'm not to be trifled with.'

'That's a very Sicilian reaction, my dear,' Baptista said.

'That feeling of rightness you had when you arrived—it was a true feeling. But it wasn't Lorenzo who caused it. It was Sicily, telling you that you'd come home.'

'What a charming theory—'

'But you believe it's just an old woman's fancy. My dear, *think*. Forget Lorenzo, and think of the land. I've seen you standing on the terrace, watching it, when you thought nobody knew. Think of it in the morning when the mist is rising, or at noon when the shadows are deep and sharp—'

'Or in the early evening when the light is that strange soft gold that happens nowhere else,' Heather mused, half to herself.

'And the language that you're learning so easily,' Baptista reminded her. 'In fact, everything about this country comes easily to you. Even the heat.'

Yes, Heather thought. She'd flowered in the sun and it had relaxed all her instincts, blurring the edges of her personality, making her feel things that otherwise...

But that was all over now. The trauma she'd suffered in the cathedral had been like a blow to the head, knocking out emotion and sensation, so that she could function calmly. With any luck it would remain that way until she returned to England, and became herself again. And what she suffered there would be nobody's business but her own.

'I'm English, Mamma,' she said now. 'I belong there.'

'No, you belong here,' Baptista said firmly. 'And you must remain.'

A shocking suspicion swept Heather. 'No! If you're thinking what I think you are—I could never marry Lorenzo now.'

'Of course not.' She stopped, alerted by a step in the corridor outside. The door opened and Heather stiffened

as she saw Lorenzo. The next moment there was a glad
cry from Baptista, and she opened her arms to her son.
He was across the room in a moment to embrace his
mother.

She tried to leave before he saw her, but at that moment
he looked up and a deep flush spread over his face. 'I'll
leave you two alone,' she said. She kissed Baptista and
departed quickly.

The little scene was over too fast for her to be aware
of feeling anything. It was only when she was walking
down the corridor that a wave of emotion swept her. Her
head might tell her that their marriage would never have
worked, but it was too soon for her to see Lorenzo without
hurt. She checked her steps and leaned against the wall,
pressing her hand against her mouth.

'Heather!' It was Renato's voice.

She looked up. 'Your brother has arrived,' she said.
'I've left them together.'

'Are you all right?'

She gave a little puzzled laugh. 'Why on earth wouldn't
I be all right? I'm going home now. Goodnight.'

It was a bad night to be thinking of lovers and honey-
moons. The full moon was exquisitely reflected in the sea,
and turned the land to pure silver. A sensible woman
would go in right now, not sit here on the terrace, thinking
of how she and her husband should be on a boat, cruising
beneath that moon, lost in each other. And she *was* a
sensible woman. It was being sensible that had enabled
her to survive the last few days.

She heard a sound behind her and turned to find
Lorenzo standing in the shadows. She sensed him take a
deep breath and straighten his shoulders before he stepped
forward.

She tried to use anticipation to suppress the pain of seeing his face, but nothing could change the fact that it was the one she'd fallen in love with, and whose smile had brightened her life.

'I've come to ask your forgiveness, and to listen to whatever you have to say to me,' he said quietly.

She raised her chin and confronted him with a bright manner. She even managed a touch of cheerfulness. 'What are you expecting?' she asked. 'A tirade crashing about your ears? Reproaches, tears—"How could you do this to me?" Let's take all that as read. I don't have the energy for a big dramatic scene.'

'But you must be angry with me.'

'Must I? Well, I suppose I am, a bit. You should have told me the truth earlier.'

'I meant to, when I came back from Stockholm, but Renato said—'

'Stop right there. The less said about Renato, the better.' After a moment she sighed. 'He's injured us both, and if there's one good thing about this mess it's that I shan't have to be related to him.' She gave an ironic laugh. 'The night we met I told him that I'd never marry you because of him. I should have stuck to that. Ah, well! I didn't. My mistake. Let's not make a tragedy of it.'

'How strong and brave you are!' he said quietly. 'You make me ashamed.'

Heather regarded him askance, a faint touch of amusement in her eyes. 'Did you expect me to go into a decline because you ran away? Don't flatter yourself. You just weren't ready for marriage, and I've got better use for my tears than to waste them on you.'

'You really don't care for me any more?'

'Luckily for us both, I don't.'

'But the night before our w—the other night—you

flung yourself into my arms and told me again and again how much you loved me—'

'That's enough,' she said sharply. 'The past is the past. Believe me, you wouldn't really want me swooning all over you and telling you that you'd broken my heart. You'd find that very uncomfortable.'

'Yes, yes, of course,' he said hastily. Then a hint of his charming smile crept over his face and he asked ruefully, 'Just the same, couldn't you flatter my vanity by being just a little bit sad?'

'Not even a little bit. Now be off with you.'

He turned to go, but stopped suddenly and said, 'If things had been different—if we'd been allowed to go at our own pace—I might not have proposed marriage just then, but when we'd parted I'd have missed you unbearably, and—'

'Stop,' she said, suddenly unable to bear any more, for this was the thought that tormented her. 'Don't talk like that. Go away, Lorenzo, please.'

'Darling—'

'Don't call me that!'

'I really was falling in love with you,' he said huskily. 'If only we'd been granted a little time—'

'Go!' she said fiercely.

She kept her face away from him, and didn't move until the fading footsteps told her that he'd gone. She was more hurt than she wanted to admit to herself. Their love was over. She could never marry Lorenzo now. But the habit of affection lingered and the misery was still sharp.

Lorenzo found both his brothers in Renato's study, pouring whisky.

'Come in,' Renato told him. 'Here.' He held out a glass.

'Thanks, I need it.' Lorenzo downed the malt in one gulp and held out his glass for more.

'You only got what you asked for,' Bernardo observed.

'Actually, I didn't. I thought it would be dreadful—tears and reproaches—'

'Then you don't know the woman you were supposed to marry,' Renato said. 'I could have told you she had more dignity than that—more dignity than you or any of us.'

'Yes, but—not a single tear, not a word of regret.'

Renato's eyes narrowed. 'By God, she knew how to deal with you!' he said softly.

'Once, I even thought she was laughing at me.'

Bernardo whistled softly. 'An exceptional woman.'

'Yes,' Renato snapped. He poured himself another full tumbler of whisky.

'Haven't you had enough?' Bernardo asked mildly.

Renato swung on him. *'Mind your own damned business!'*

Bernardo shrugged. 'It's nothing to me. But it's not like you to drink heavily—'

'Well, tonight I feel like drinking the cellar dry.'

'You're the one she's mad at,' Lorenzo told him. 'She blames the whole thing on you, and she's right. If you'd kept out of our affairs, who knows what might have happened?'

'Spare me the happy ever after ending,' Renato sneered. 'I'm not convinced.'

'Well, I am,' Lorenzo said with a flash of anger.

'You're out of your mind. It's much too late for second thoughts.'

'You wouldn't like to take a little bet on that, would you? Heather knows we'd have been all right, but for you.

And we might be yet. She's a wonderful woman, and maybe it isn't too late—'

He got no further. Renato's hands were around his throat, choking the life out of him. Renato's eyes, close to his, were glittering, filled with murder.

'*Renato, for God's sake stop!*' That was Bernardo, hauling him off, having to use all his strength, holding him back while Lorenzo choked.

'Get out of here,' Renato raged. 'Get out of my sight!'

'Be damned to you!' Lorenzo said hoarsely. 'Why didn't you stay out of my affairs?'

'Get out, for God's sake!' Bernardo told him. 'You two killing each other is all we need.'

Lorenzo flung Renato a bitter look and departed. Bernardo kept a cautious hold on his brother until the door was closed.

'Oh, the hell with it! Let me go,' Renato said. Bernardo did so at once. 'What are you doing here, anyway? Why aren't you with your lady?'

'I can wait,' Bernardo said. 'She's worth waiting for.'

'Don't tell me this family's actually going to have a wedding after all?'

'I think so. But that's for your ears alone.' Bernardo gave one of his rare smiles. 'As the family head, do you approve?'

'Would you take any notice if I didn't?'

'I'd mind. It wouldn't stop me.'

'For what it's worth, you have my blessing. You're a fortunate man.'

'I know. I can't really believe it. I keep waiting for the snag that will ruin everything.'

'There's no snag.' Renato added quietly, 'One of us, at least, is going to be lucky in love.'

They chinked glasses. Then Bernardo said uneasily,
'Lorenzo is still our brother.'

'I know that.'

'I think you should be careful.'

'Of him?'

'No. Of yourself. Goodnight.'

He went without another word, leaving Renato alone,
wishing he could get rid of the tension that plagued him.
He poured most of his whisky back into the bottle, knowing that wasn't the answer. Nor was sleep the answer.

He slammed his hand down, realising that there was no
answer. There hadn't been one since that evening when
he'd met a young woman who'd told him to jump in the
river. He'd admired her, been amused by her, but he was
so used to planning his life as he wished that he hadn't
seen the danger, and had actually encouraged her to marry
his brother.

The danger had come in a blinding flash when it was
far too late: just before the wedding, when no man of
honour could make a move. She'd touched his heart with
her vulnerability, an experience so strange that he'd been
thrown off balance. And in that confused, blinded state
he'd offered her his brotherly help. After that his hands
had been tied.

In the cathedral it seemed that Lorenzo had solved the
problem. Except that there still echoed through his head
the tormenting memory of a young woman, a few hours
before what should have been her wedding, her voice carrying sweetly on the night air.

'I just wanted to say how much I love you—love you—
love you—'

Women had always fallen in love with Lorenzo, and
stayed in love with him, long after hope was gone. It
wasn't just his looks or his easy good nature. It was a

mysterious 'something' that wouldn't let them go, like a magic spell. Renato had never begrudged him before.

And some men, he thought, were just the opposite, as though they carried a curse. Suddenly he saw his mother's agonised face as it had been when he came round after the bike accident. Other faces followed——Heather reading the letter in the cathedral, her love gone, her career destroyed; his mother again, distraught and fainting; even Lorenzo, pale and ashamed at what he'd been driven to do.

All hurt because of himself, because he destroyed whatever he touched.

CHAPTER SEVEN

IT WAS time for Angie to leave. She'd remained a few extra days to support her friend, but now she must leave for England and her work. But surely, Heather thought, she would return to Sicily soon, because she couldn't bear to be away from Bernardo.

She knew this was no light o' love. It had a depth and intensity that she'd never seen in Angie before. Once she'd surprised them in each other's arms, heard the husky murmur of Bernardo's voice speaking words of eternal passion and devotion, and crept quickly away. But the time had passed with no announcement, and yesterday they had both vanished. Of course, they were making plans, Heather thought, and before Angie left they would announce their engagement.

But when she went into their room she knew that something was badly wrong. Angie was packing her suitcase with a kind of fierce purpose, and her face was set in a way that meant she was determined not to cry. In that expression Heather recognised her own experience.

'Darling, what is it?' she asked, taking Angie by the shoulders. 'Have you quarrelled with Bernardo?'

'Oh, no, we haven't quarrelled,' Angie said bitterly. 'There's nothing to quarrel about. He just explained to me calmly and reasonably why he'd *die* rather than marry me.'

'But—he adores you, anyone can see that. What can be wrong if you love each other?'

'That's what I thought, but love isn't enough. He says

102

he loves me. He says he'll never love any other woman, but it's impossible.'

'But—*why*?'

In halting words Angie told to her why she was planning to go away and leave the man her heart was set on, and whose heart was set on her. She explained it badly, because she was distraught from the day she'd spent with her lover, trying to understand why he was determined on a parting that would break both their hearts—his as well as hers, he'd left her in no doubt of it. But all her love, all her logic, her arguments and frantic pleading, had made no dent on his iron-hard resolution. He might suffer for it until his last moment, but he would not marry her.

'I can't follow that,' Heather said at last. 'To let such a thing come between you—in this day and age.'

'Bernardo's a Sicilian,' Angie said a little wildly. 'He doesn't belong in this day and age. And the bottom line is that his pride means more to him than I do. So I'm leaving. And please Heather, can we not talk about it any more, because I don't think I could stand it?'

Heather didn't answer in words, but she drew her friend close, and they clung to each other.

'How about coming with me?' Angie asked huskily.

'I can't leave yet, not until Baptista is better. But I'll be home soon.'

'I'll keep your room for you.' She gave a wonky smile. 'We haven't either of us had much luck with Sicilian men, have we?'

Heather would have gone with her to the airport, but Bernardo was taking her, so she backed off to give them a last few moments alone together, hoping his mind would change. Perhaps he would even bring Angie home with him.

But he returned alone, with a face of flint. He met

Heather's attempts to talk with courtesy, but it was clear that he'd built a wall around himself. He stayed only long enough for a word with Baptista, before driving away to his home in the mountains, and remaining there.

'What's the matter with him?' Heather stormed to Renato. 'It was as good as settled.'

'I'm as taken aback as you are. Only a few days ago he was set on marrying her. He told me so. But then he made this discovery, and it changed everything.'

'Talk to him, for pity's sake!'

'I have no influence with Bernardo. We had different mothers, and that matters. We have a saying in Sicily. "A man's mother is his soul. If he loses her, he will never find her again." Bernardo feels that if he marries Angie he will lose his soul.'

'Then he's a fool,' Heather said fiercely.

'We're all fools about the one woman who matters.'

'How would you know?' she asked scornfully. 'No woman has ever mattered that much to you.'

'True. And when I watch my brothers I'm glad of it.'

'Yes, you protect yourself from being hurt, don't you?' She sighed. 'Well, you're probably wise. I must try to learn your way. I think it has a lot to be said for it.'

'No, don't do that,' he said unexpectedly. 'It would make you less than yourself, and you mustn't be. These last few days you've been stronger than any of us.'

She shrugged. 'That's because I've lost the power to feel. It's a great advantage. You know yourself how convenient it makes life. We're the lucky ones, Renato. We won't suffer as Angie and Bernardo are doing. Other people, yes, but not us.'

He took her arm to stop her turning away. 'Whatever you do, don't become like me.'

His fingers were touching her bare skin, but she felt no

reaction. How ironically now she recalled the flashes of desire for him that had tormented her before the wedding. All gone now. Dust and ashes. Like her heart.

'But you're the way to be,' she said lightly. 'I envy you.'

His grip tightened. 'Why, because you think I've lost the power to feel? You're wrong. Sometimes I wish—' She felt the tremor that passed through him. He released her.

'No matter,' he said curtly. 'I'll talk to Bernardo, but it won't do any good.'

The day after her return from hospital Baptista summoned Renato and Heather to her presence, like a queen granting an audience.

Heather was reluctant to attend. She was in a strange mood. After several nights of sleeping badly, the armour of unfeeling calm that had protected her so far was beginning to crack. Through the weak places she could glimpse the storm of misery and anger that would overtake her if she gave it a chance.

Worse still were the moments when everything seemed bitterly funny. If she gave way to those she knew she would collapse in wild, uncontrollable laughter. But she mustn't let that happen, so she buckled the armour on more firmly than ever, and hoped for the best.

Baptista had left her bed and was reclining in state on a sofa in her grand sitting room. She looked them both over as they appeared before her, taking up positions at some distance apart.

'We can't leave things like this,' she announced. 'It's all been handled very badly.'

'Perhaps Lorenzo should be here,' Renato suggested.

'Lorenzo is the past. It's the future that concerns me.'

'We know what that has to be,' Heather told her. 'I'll return Bella Rosaria to you—'

'That must wait. If you give it back in the same tax year as I gave it to you, we run into all sorts of problems. We haven't yet discussed what happened in the cathedral.'

Heather took a sharp breath. 'How can there be anything to say? It's over.'

'Over? When such an insult was offered you by my family?'

'That "insult" talk is old-fashioned—' she protested.

'And Sicily is an old-fashioned place, even now. If such a thing had happened to me my father would have shot the man dead. And there wouldn't even have been a trial.'

'Well, I'm not going to start shooting,' Heather declared. She was trying to lighten the atmosphere, but she couldn't resist adding, 'Not Lorenzo, anyway.'

'I sympathise with your feelings, my daughter,' Baptista said, giving Renato a look that would have frozen the blood of a less courageous man. He met it with a grimace in which affection was mixed with hearty respect. It amused Heather to realise that, however he treated anyone else, Renato trod very carefully with his mother.

'Lorenzo and I have already met and declared a truce,' she said.

'And I'm grateful, but that isn't the end of the matter. You have been injured by my family, and you cannot be allowed to suffer.'

'Well, if Renato uses his influence with Gossways to restore me to the training programme, I won't have suffered.'

Renato frowned. 'And that's really your idea of recompense?'

'It'll put me back where I was before you entered my

life,' she said firmly. 'I'll be able to pretend you don't exist. In other words, the perfect solution.'

'Thank you!' he snapped.

'Don't mention it.'

'It's not enough,' Baptista said. 'There is the dishonour.'

'But I told you, Lorenzo's actions can't dishonour me.'

'They can dishonour his family,' Baptista said, so fiercely that Heather was startled. 'He insulted you, and the whole family will bear the shame of it until we have made amends.'

'I won't marry him now.'

'Certainly not. But I have another son. I agree he's done little to recommend himself to you, but Renato is to blame for this and Renato must put it right.' Baptista spoke in her most regal manner. 'Your marriage should take place immediately.'

There was one moment's total, thunderstruck silence. Heather tried to speak but couldn't. The control she'd struggled for was slipping away, releasing the crazy laughter that had been fighting to get out. She gave a choke and turned aside swiftly with her hand over her mouth. But it was useless. A bubble was rising inside her, shooting up until it reached the outside world in peal after peal of mirth. The whole thing was mad. It could only have been imagined in this society that followed its own rules and cared for no other.

'I'm sorry,' she gasped at last, 'but that's the funniest thing you could have said. Me? Marry Renato? A man I can't endure the sight of? Oh, heavens!' She went off into another paroxysm.

Renato regarded her with hard eyes. Then he began to speak in a low, outraged voice. He spoke in Sicilian and Heather couldn't follow it, but she managed to pick out the words for 'crazy', 'unbelievable' and something that she guessed meant 'not in a million years'.

'That's just how I feel, too,' she told him. 'Oh, dear! Don't get me started again.'

'In my day a young woman knew better than to laugh at an eligible match,' Baptista said with haughty disapproval.

'But Renato isn't an eligible match,' Heather pointed out when she'd managed to calm down a little. 'One, he doesn't want to marry anyone. Two, he doesn't want to marry *me*. Three, hell will freeze over before I marry him. It's out of the question.'

'It's good sense. You came here to marry a son of this house, and that's what you must do. Then things will be right again.'

'They'd be very far from right,' Heather said desperately. 'I don't know how you can have thought of such a thing—the last man in the world I'd ever—'

'The feeling is mutual,' Renato said coldly. 'Mamma, I have the greatest respect for you, but you must forget this idea.'

'Your feelings don't enter into it,' Baptista told him firmly. 'You have injured a decent young woman, and must make reparation.'

'One phone call to Gossways will do that very nicely, thank you,' Heather said crisply.

'I'll make it at once,' Renato declared. 'Plus I'll pay all your expenses for your trip here and—'

'Renato, I'm warning you, if you *dare* offer me money you'll be very sorry.'

'I'm already sorry: sorry I ever met you, sorry my brother met you, sorry we welcomed you into our home—'

'Then it's a pity you took so much trouble to get me

here, isn't it? When I got up to walk out of the restaurant in London you should have let me go.'

'If I had, you'd have gone under that car.'

'If I hadn't been running away from you I'd have been in no danger from the car.'

'If you'd been a more reasonable woman you wouldn't have been running away.'

'*I*—? If *I'd* been—? You have a very selective memory. You looked me up and down like a piece of merchandise, decided that I'd just about do, and awarded me your brand of approval. For which you had the nerve to expect me to be grateful. As for poor Lorenzo—remember Lorenzo? The groom?—he didn't know whether he was coming or going.'

'I understood that he proposed to you in the hospital.'

'Only after your majesty made your wishes known. Then we were all supposed to fall into line, weren't we? The way everybody always has for you. The way I'm supposed to today. Only you've miscalculated now, just as you did then. I won't marry you, Renato, and you know why? Because after the way you've behaved you're not good enough. And if the angel Gabriel came down off a cloud with a signed testimonial I would still say you're not good enough.'

'Indeed!' Renato snapped. 'Then allow me to remind you that in Sicily, as, I believe, in other parts of the world, it's normal for a woman *to wait until she's received a proposal of marriage before rejecting it.*'

'I was simply trying to save time.'

'You shouldn't have bothered. Then I wouldn't have needed to say that I would rather swim the Straits of Messina in lead weights than link my life to a woman who is nothing but trouble.'

'Then we're agreed and everything's—oh, Mamma, I'm sorry!'

Shocked, Heather had just remembered Baptista's frail condition, but the old woman was watching them both, bright-eyed, with something that might almost have been enjoyment.

'Yes, I'm sorry too,' Renato said. 'We had no right to lose our tempers—your heart—'

'My heart is well, but you are both being very foolish. I advise you to reconsider.'

'Never.' They spoke with one voice.

'Very well. Perhaps I raised the subject in the wrong way.'

'Mamma, there's no way you could raise this subject that would make Renato acceptable,' Heather pleaded. 'I don't want to marry him, I want to kick his shins.'

'You're perfectly right,' Baptista said at once. 'I never saw a man who needed it more. When you're his wife you can do it every day.'

'This is my mother talking?' Renato enquired grimly.

'I'm not blind to your faults, my son,' Baptista retorted. 'I've found you the perfect wife, someone who won't hurry to agree with you and say, "Yes dear, no dear!" In short, someone who sees right through you to the other side, and isn't impressed by what she sees.'

'That's certainly true,' Heather observed. 'But while I'm reforming Renato's character—and, heaven knows, he needs it—how do *I* benefit?'

'You get to stay here,' Baptista told her. 'You become part of this family, and a Sicilian, both of which nature meant you to be.'

'That's the most tempting thing you've said to me so far,' Heather said. She was recovering her poise and even a touch of humour. 'If you could fix the last two without my having to burden myself with Renato, I'd be delighted.'

'No pleasure comes without pain, my dear. You'll learn to put up with him.'

Heather leaned over and kissed Baptista's cheek. 'Sorry, Mamma. The price is too high.'

'Much too high,' Renato agreed. 'Let us forget it was ever mentioned.' He too had calmed down, although anger still lurked far back in his dark eyes.

'In that case, go away,' Baptista said, seeming to tire of the subject. 'But before you leave, Renato, you can pour me a large brandy.'

Later that day Bernardo returned and went straight to see Baptista. He was calm but very pale, and he politely declined the chance to discuss his troubles. She knew better than to press him.

'Never mind,' she said kindly. 'Things will work out. They usually do. And there's one thing to look forward to. Heather and Renato are going to get married.'

Midnight in the garden. Here, at least, there was the chance for Heather to be at peace, wandering along winding paths, breathing in the scents of a hundred flowers. Here were the rose bushes, created from cuttings from the original garden at Bella Rosaria. She understood so much better now, a symbol of a love that had never died, despite the contentment of an arranged marriage. That was the kind of love she'd wanted, the kind she'd believed she had. And Baptista wanted her to settle for less. She'd thought she'd come to terms with the sadness, but this was a new sadness, showing her the bleak path her life might yet take.

She sat on the stone edge of the fountain and looked

down into the water, seeing the dark shadow of her own head and the silver moon behind. She trailed her fingers, shattering the moon to a thousand fragments, and when the water grew still again, there was another head beside hers.

'You shouldn't have been put through that,' Renato said. 'Mamma gets carried away sometimes. I'm sorry for the things I said—'

'I suppose I was just as bad. There's no point in having a go at you anyway. It's over and done with. I said you were too ready to arrange people's lives, but now I see where you get it from.'

'Don't be angry with her.'

'I'm not. I think she's sweet. But, honestly, what an absurd idea!' She gave a small choke.

'Yes, you've made it clear that you find it funny,' he said with a slight edge in his voice.

'I'm sorry, I'm not laughing at you. It's just—everything—all at once—'

She tried to pull herself together, but suddenly she couldn't stop. She'd thought she'd exorcised the wild mood that had possessed her earlier, but now it was back, worse than ever. Sobs of laughter rose up in her, one after the other, each one bigger than the last, until they weren't laughter any more, and all the tears she'd been suppressing forced their way out.

'That's enough,' Renato said, laying a hand on her shoulder. Then he paused because he could feel the shuddering of her body, and knew that it had changed. 'You're not crying after all this time, surely?'

She tried to say, 'No, of course not,' but the words came out huskily, and then she couldn't manage words at all. She'd controlled herself so fiercely that now she had no control left. She was mortified at Renato seeing her like this but she couldn't do anything about it.

'Heather—' he said quietly.

'No—it's nothing—I'm all right, I just need to—'

'You just need to cry it out,' he said. 'Heather—Heather, listen—' He sat beside her on the fountain and laid light hands on her shoulders and gave her a little shake. 'Stop trying to be so damned strong all the time.'

'I've got to be strong,' she said. 'I'm among sharks.'

'Not really. I'm the only shark, and I'm not biting tonight. Just for once, let's forget that you hate me.'

'I don't—know how.'

'Well, that's honest,' he said, gathering her into his arms. 'Hate me, then, but let's call a truce.'

She couldn't reply. Anguish had taken hold of her completely. She'd told herself that it didn't hurt, but it did. All the happiness she'd dared to enjoy now turned on her, transformed to grief and bitterness. It swamped her, engulfed her, and there was no help or comfort in the world, except, mysteriously, for her enemy, whose arms enfolded her.

He held her tightly, murmuring words of kindness that her ears hardly heard, although her heart discerned them, and eased a little. It made no sense, but there was something about his voice that warmed her and made everything seem not quite so bad. He drew away to look at her, brushing back the hair from her face with gentle fingers.

'I didn't think you could ever cry,' he said huskily. 'You were so good at shutting us all out of your feelings—or maybe just me—'

Her tears still flowed, but his soft caresses against her features were making the jagged edges of the world recede and the misery soften.

'Nothing is worth your tears,' he murmured. He laid

his lips against her wet cheeks, then her eyes. 'Don't cry—*please*.'

She grew completely still, listening to his soft words and letting her body relax against him. With one hand he stroked her hair while his lips wandered over her face. She thought perhaps she shouldn't do this, but the thought was far away, muffled by the warm sweetness that was taking possession of her. She knew that at any moment his lips would find her mouth, and the breath came faster in her throat as she waited for it to happen.

When it did his touch was so light that she had to reach up to him to be sure, slipping an arm about his neck, cupping his head with her hand. It was only a few hours since they'd quarrelled, and soon they would probably quarrel again, but now all the world was upside down, and it seemed natural to let him hold her close while his lips continued the work of consolation.

'Renato...' she whispered, not knowing if she were protesting or simply asking a question.

'Hush! Why should we always be fighting?'

She didn't want to fight a man who could hold her so tenderly. She still didn't trust him, but somehow that didn't matter so much now. What did matter was the slow movement of his mouth across hers, and the sense of sweet contentment that pervaded her.

Her mouth was caressing him back, seeking new sensations. She wanted more of him. He was dangerous, but since coming to this country she'd discovered that she responded to the thrill of danger. She put up her hand and laid it against his hair, thick and springy against her palm. Then his cheek. He needed a shave. That was Renato, not smooth and appealing, but all rough edges and sharp angles. You had to take him as you found him. He couldn't be trusted, but sometimes he could be wonderful.

He slackened his hold, but kept his arms in place, resting his lips against her hair. He was trembling as much as she.

'You said once—I could always ask you for a brother's help,' she reminded him huskily.

'I remember. But neither of us knew this day would come.'

Hadn't they? she thought wildly. Hadn't they?

'Keep your word now,' she whispered. 'Help me as a brother. Help me find my place back in England so that I can go home and forget I ever came to Sicily.'

'Will you forget us so easily?'

He would have held her but she disengaged herself and backed away, trying to put a safe distance between them. But how far was safe?

'Don't ask me that, Renato. You know I can't answer. Just help me go home. That's all I want.'

CHAPTER EIGHT

IT WAS Baptista's idea that Heather should visit Bella Rosaria. 'It's time you were looking over your property,' she said. 'But come to see me often.'

The suggestion appealed to Heather. She could never regard the estate as hers, but while matters were being sorted out it would be the ideal place to stay.

She took a car from the garage and drove out of Palermo, taking the winding road that led up to the village of Ellona, and the pink stone villa that dominated it. It was mid-morning and as she climbed she saw how the fresh, vivid light sharpened the contours of the land, which was freshly harvested and brown after the long, fierce summer. She realised that already she was thinking like a Sicilian. Baptista had been right. She loved this place and didn't want to leave it.

Baptista must have telephoned ahead, because when Heather reached the villa she found they were ready for her. Jocasta, the housekeeper, had prepared the best room in readiness for the new mistress. It was dark and old-fashioned, with crimson tiles on the floor and furniture made of wood that was almost black. But everything was luxurious, and the huge bed was the most comfortable she'd ever known.

She met her steward, Luigi, a small, fierce man, brown as a berry, who might have been any age from fifty to eighty, and who offered to show her over her property. He spoke in a mixture of Sicilian and English. Heather responded in the same do-it-yourself dialect, and they understood each other perfectly.

The villa had its own stables with three horses. Heather had learned to ride while visiting Angie, and now she set out for a ride over the countryside, accompanied by Luigi. Everywhere the land was changing, reflecting the passing of summer and the start of the wet season. Luigi explained that it had been a good harvest this year. She would do well. He didn't seem to notice that she was sunk in embarrassment.

For her first evening Jocasta had ordered what she called 'a simple meal', which turned out to be aubergine salad, followed by squid and macaroni stew, followed by liver with wine sauce. The ride had left her with a good appetite and she had no difficulty doing justice to all these dishes, plus the caramelised oranges. She had the satisfaction of knowing that she'd delighted Jocasta's husband Gino, who did the cooking and was hovering just outside the door. The whole was washed down with half a bottle of a light rosé called Donnafugata, after which she went to bed and slept like a baby.

A strange, dream-like calm seemed to descend on her. The sense of being in limbo was stronger than ever, but now it was a pleasant limbo where she had nothing to do but discover the extent of her new found power. The strained nerves that had betrayed her to Renato in the garden were recovering from their collapse, growing stronger every day.

Some long rides did her good, and her spirits began to be normal again. She made several visits to the Residenza, always choosing a time when Renato was unlikely to be there. To her relief Baptista didn't raise the dangerous subject again. They would talk and discuss Bella Rosaria as though it really was hers. Baptista was full of wise suggestions which Heather duly passed on to Luigi. She was determined to do no more, but little by little she found herself fascinated by the running of the estate.

She wondered what Renato thought of her flight, or the way she'd taken possession of the place he had wanted to own, according to Lorenzo. Doubtless he would soon come storming to visit her. She was ready for him, unafraid.

But when days passed with no sign of him she knew a sense of anticlimax. Then she grew irked at his offhand way of treating her. Something had been left unresolved between them and it had to be sorted. Why couldn't he see that?

It was obvious now that she'd always known he would kiss her. From the moment he walked into Gossways everything he'd said or done had been the actions of a man who would kiss her one day. Her reactions had been clouded by her honest belief that she'd been in love with another man. But behind the curtain of that belief she'd felt like a woman who expected—wanted—to be kissed.

They had almost come to grief the day on the boat, and by the time of the ball her mistake had been staring her in the face. After the aborted wedding she'd retreated into herself, wanting nothing to do with him. But when he'd taken her into his arms by the fountain she'd come to life again so urgently that it had alarmed her. She'd fled because she needed time to think, but now she had to meet him again, and see how he looked when he saw her.

But he didn't appear. Lorenzo seemed almost permanently abroad now, but one day Baptista remarked casually that Renato too was away. She was feeling rather lonely with neither of her sons there, but wasn't it delightful that the two of them could enjoy some time alone together? In a colourless voice Heather agreed that it was.

Bernardo came to ask if there was anything he could do for her. He looked ill and wretched, so Heather took pity on him, invited him to dinner and spent the time talking about Angie, who'd written twice. He said little, but she sensed that he was alive to every mention of Angie's name. She knew that feeling of being haunted. Something of her sympathy must have shown in her manner, for by the end of the evening they were excellent friends.

It would have been tempting to drift forever in this pleasant no-man's-land, but she forced herself to telephone Gossways. As she'd feared, her place on the training programme had gone for ever. She could return as a sales assistant, but two grades lower than when she'd left. Renato had made no call on her behalf.

So that was that.

It was another week before she saw Renato's car winding its way up the narrow main street of Ellona one afternoon, just as the sun was setting. About time too, she thought as she descended the stone steps outside the villa. She tried to arrange her face to suggest the right combination of welcome and reserve.

But it wasn't Renato.

'Hello,' Lorenzo called cheerily, bounding out and waving as though nothing was wrong between them. 'I came to see how you were.'

It took a moment to pull herself together and seem normal. How could it be Lorenzo when it should have been Renato? How dared he come here when his brother didn't?

'Fine,' she said, smiling. 'I like it here.'

'All on your own?'

'There are worse things than being alone. Come inside.'

He bounded up the steps, an attractive figure in his light brown trousers and blue short-sleeved shirt, open at the throat. He was smiling and seemed not to have a care in the world. That should have hurt. But it didn't. Those feelings already seemed long in the past.

'I brought you a housewarming present,' he said, flourishing an elegantly wrapped parcel. It turned out to be an alabaster head in the style of a Greek goddess. It was about ten inches tall, delicately made and charming.

'It's a reproduction of a piece in a museum,' Lorenzo explained. 'I chose it because she looks like you. Actually, I'll confess, I bought it for you weeks ago. After what happened—I wasn't sure how to give it to you. But as a housewarming gift—' He gave a deprecating shrug. He was full of charm.

'I love it,' she said. 'And I know just the right place for it.'

She led him out to the rose garden, where there was a little alcove that she'd thought was rather bare. To her delight it harmonised perfectly.

'Lovely,' Lorenzo agreed. 'Do you like this spot, then? I know it's always been a favorite place of Mamma's.'

Perhaps he didn't know the story of Fede, the rose grower. Heather wondered if Baptista would mind if she hinted at it, but Lorenzo's next words killed the impulse. 'Don't you find the house rather gloomy? I always did.'

'Gloomy? Not at all. It's cool and peaceful. I love it.'

'We always had to spend a few weeks here in the summer. I just remember longing to get away.'

So much for her dream of living here with him. A fantasy, born of ignorance, like so many of her thoughts of Lorenzo, she realised. If they had known each other longer she would have seen her infatuation for what it was.

They had wine on the terrace overlooking the garden. Lorenzo was looking mischievous. 'I heard about the row,' he said.

'Row?' she asked cautiously.

'Come on, everyone knows what happened. Mamma tried to arrange a match between you and Renato and you just roared with laughter. I wish I'd been there to see that. My brother, who spends most of his time dodging traps by determined women, actually getting the cold shoulder.'

'It wasn't like that at all,' Heather said firmly. 'Renato and I both felt that it wasn't a good idea.' How dull and prim the words sounded against the explosive reality. But it was best that way. Whatever she might feel about Renato she wasn't going to offer him up for Lorenzo's amusement.

'I'm sure *you* don't like the idea, but *him*? For one thing, you've got this place.'

'Which I'm giving back as soon as the paperwork's sorted.'

'Plus you turned him down. Who do you think was the last woman who did that?'

Me, Heather thought, remembering how she'd told Renato to jump in the river on the first evening.

'Refused him before he'd even asked,' Lorenzo went on with a grin. 'I'll bet that got under his skin. He's been in a foul temper ever since he got back from America. Careful! You nearly spilled your drink.'

He was back, she thought. And he hadn't called her.

Well, why should he?

Because he had no right to leave her on hot coals.

Hell would freeze over before she asked when he'd returned.

'Let's drop this subject,' she said. 'I'm not going to marry Renato.'

'I wouldn't care to take a wager on that. You laughed at him. He can't just ignore that.'

'What are you saying? That he'll try to win me over to save his pride?'

'I wouldn't put it past him. He's not used to having to win a woman over. Usually they're only too willing.'

She didn't answer and he gave a rueful half-smile. 'We could have made it, you know—if he hadn't interfered.'

'We'll never know,' she told him. 'It's in the past. Over.'

But he laid down his wineglass on the stone balustrade and reached out to draw her into his arms. Heather had half expected it, and she allowed it to happen because there was something she wanted to know. She even kissed him back. Not out of love. Or passion. Curiosity.

Once she'd loved him so much. The sweetness of his kisses had transported her to heaven. Or so she'd thought. But heaven had turned out to be a rather narrow cul-de-sac. A kiss should open up infinite vistas of joy and passion, even when it was gentle, hovering on the verge of passion, but uncommitted, so that you yearned for...

She sighed and freed herself. It had been a useful experiment and she'd learned what she wanted to know. Lorenzo was basically a pleasant young man, but he still had some growing up to do. It had been like kissing cardboard.

Then she turned her head and saw Renato, regarding them sardonically.

'Forgive me,' he said. 'I didn't realise the two of you would be occupied.'

'Then you should have done,' Lorenzo said cheekily.

Renato advanced and took his arm. 'You were just leaving.'

'Was I?'

'No,' Heather said, furious at this high-handedness. 'I'd just invited Lorenzo to lunch, and he'd accepted.'

Lorenzo caught Renato's eye and what he saw there seemed to decide him. 'Perhaps another time,' he said.

Even knowing it was futile, Heather made an attempt to assert herself as mistress of her own home. 'Not another time,' she said firmly. 'Now. Gino will have prepared food for two—'

'Don't worry, I'm hungry,' Renato said. He regarded Lorenzo with surprise. 'Are you still here?'

'Just going,' Lorenzo said. But he deposited a cheeky kiss on Heather's cheek before vanishing.

When they were alone she turned on Renato, who was looking at her coldly. She even thought she detected a hint of scorn in his eyes, and her temper rose to meet it.

'You've got an unspeakable nerve!' she told him.

'My apologies,' he said, not sounding at all apologetic. 'But I wanted to be rid of him and that was the quickest way.'

'And what about what *I* wanted?'

'It's fairly obvious what you wanted. *Nome de dio*, I thought you had more dignity!'

'How dare you?'

'Oh, please! You were being pretty obvious. No doubt the first step to luring him upstairs to bed.'

She gasped, and would have struck out if he hadn't caught her wrist. 'No, don't attack me just because I speak plainly. If your aim was to get Lorenzo back to the altar, you won't do it that way.'

She was angry enough to speak without thinking. 'If

I'd wanted to trap Lorenzo by taking him to bed I'd have done it before now.'

His grip tightened, and there was a strange light in his eyes. 'Are you saying you never did?'

She drew a sharp breath. 'Let go of me at once.'

'I wondered if you'd slept with him—you denied it the day we met, or I thought you did—but I could be wrong— tell me—' There was a flash of anger in his eyes. *'Tell me!'*

'I'll tell you nothing. It's none of your business.'

'The best thing Lorenzo did was running off that day. He'd have disappointed you. You know that, don't you?'

She did know. The beating of her heart told her, but she wouldn't admit it to him. 'If you thought that, it's a pity you pushed me into his arms,' she said.

'I didn't know then. Neither of us knew. But we know now. He'd have let you down, and then—'

'And then—?'

He didn't need to answer, but it was there between them. And then she would have turned to him.

'Never,' she whispered. 'Never. If I was Lorenzo's wife, I'd have been faithful to the very end.'

'To the bitter end,' he corrected.

'If necessary.'

'No matter how bitter the end would have been for all of us?' His voice became cruel. 'We could all have burned in a self-made hell for all you cared.'

'You needn't have. You have other diversions.'

'Sometimes they're not—' He became aware of what he was saying and stopped abruptly. 'Shall I tell you what hell is?' he asked after a moment.

'I'm sure you know many kinds.'

'It's to love without desire, and desire without love.'

She drew a shuddering breath. 'Let me go, Renato. Let me go now. You have no right to do this.'

She wrenched her wrist free and backed away. But she kept her eyes on him as she would have done a wild animal that might spring either way. This was Renato, a man it was always safest to treat as an enemy. He was still in a state of suppressed anger, his face paler than she had ever seen it, and she knew his control could slip at any moment.

And then Jocasta's step outside the door brought them both out of the fevered dream and they turned forced smiles on her. Somehow the jagged air settled back to normal, leaving only unbelievable memories behind.

Renato greeted Jocasta like an old friend and Heather could see how delighted the housekeeper was to see him. As they exchanged some backchat in Sicilian she mentally stood back, trying not to be aware that she was tingling and newly alive after their brief exchange. Once again they were fighting within a few minutes of meeting, but with Renato fighting held an excitement all its own.

Like Lorenzo, Renato was dressed informally in a short-sleeved shirt, open at the throat, but on him the effect was different. Lorenzo blended into his surroundings. Renato stood out from them. His vital masculinity made him always more noticeable than anything else. Heather found her anger slipping away. He'd been gone so long, and the little ache that had been in her breast for days was explained now, hard though she found it to admit to herself.

'Your favorite wine, *signore*,' Jocasta said, pouring for him.

'Good. And I've had a pressing invitation to lunch,' he said shamelessly.

'Then I'll tell Gino to prepare some meatballs in tomato soup,' Jocasta said.

'Not for lunch, because they'll take time to prepare and we'd like to eat quickly before we go out,' Renato said. 'But I'll have them for supper tonight.'

'I never invited you for lunch or supper,' Heather pointed out when they were alone.

'But you were just about to. I could tell.'

To think she'd actually been glad to see him! He seemed to ruffle her feathers for the devilment of it. Why couldn't it have been him in the car this afternoon, as it should have been? But no, he had to arrive at the wrong moment, teasing and tormenting her, putting her on the defensive, ruining what might have been a delightful visit. And doing all this while looking so vividly alive that something sang inside her and she wondered how she had endured so long without the sight of him. She could gladly have wrung his neck.

'And as for telling her when to serve lunch—'

'We're going out straight after and there's no time to waste.'

As they sat down to lunch they had each managed to slide the polite masks into place, and Renato had done more. He managed to look as though the whole scene hadn't taken place. Heather only hoped her own efforts were as successful.

'Tell me, how have you been while I've been away?' he asked.

'I've enjoyed your absence considerably. Can I hope to have it repeated again soon?'

'Not for a while, I'm afraid. This estate has always been one of our most productive, and it has to stay that way. That means you must know what to do. Luigi will take responsibility, of course, but if you don't know what he's doing he won't respect you.'

'But—' Heather meant to explain yet again that she was going to return the estate to its rightful owner, but gave up. Nobody had listened to her so far, and plainly Renato wasn't listening now.

In fact he seemed to regard her chiefly as an audience. He talked at her rather than to her, and once remarked that she wasn't listening properly. He was totally businesslike and the electricity that had flashed between them earlier might never have been.

'The rains are due,' he told her. 'But with any luck we'll have a few days first. That's why I'm here now. Let's go.'

A small crowd had gathered to watch them get into his open-topped car at the front of the villa. 'Your tenants,' Renato told her.

'You mean some of them live in houses that belong to the estate?'

'All of them live in Ellona, which is yours.'

'But I thought—just one or two houses—'

'Every house in the village. That's why they're watching you. What you do affects them.'

That was only the start. As they drove out that afternoon he showed her vineyards, orchards and olive groves that were all hers. Everything was well kept and flourishing, the tenants celebrating bumper harvests, eager to talk about loans for next year's fertiliser. This was Renato's territory, and Heather had expected him to use his expert knowledge to reduce her to silence. But she had to admit that he behaved beautifully, bringing her into every conversation, treating her with respect, explaining what she needed to know without talking down to her.

At one sheep farm she became fascinated, asking a se-

ries of intelligent questions that had the tenant family nod-
ding approval. In a combination of English, Italian and
Sicilian she explained that her uncle had been a shepherd.

'We used to spend holidays with him and he'd let me
help with the lambing. I loved that.'

'What kind of sheep?' they wanted to know.

'Blackface, some angora—' And she was away, talking
eagerly.

They took her to see their best ram and watched as she
ran knowledgeable hands over it. They discussed vets'
bills. Scandalous. And milking. Did they milk their sheep?
They did but they hadn't expected her to know it was
possible.

At last the talk died. She looked around and found them
staring at her with interest. Renato was smiling as though
he'd won something. Heather felt a prickle on her spine
as a suspicion came to her.

As they drove back through Ellona Heather's suspi-
cions increased. Every window and door in the main street
was open, and they were being studied by curious eyes.
The plump little priest stepped out to hail them, and they
stopped at his house for a drink. When they emerged they
were watched even more intently. It was obvious that this
scrutiny had a reason, and she was beginning to fear that
she knew what it was.

As they reached the villa Renato said, 'Tomorrow we'll
go on horseback.'

'You're coming back tomorrow?'

'I'm staying overnight. You don't mind, do you?'

'Not at all,' she said politely. 'I'll tell Jocasta.'

'No need. I should think she's put my things in my
room by now.'

He was right. Clearly he was a favourite with Jocasta,
who had not only unpacked his case but ordered the eve-

ning meal to suit him. Heather didn't know how to protest about the way he'd taken over. After all, she kept saying that Bella Rosaria wasn't really hers, so it was hard to complain when he took her at her word.

They enjoyed the last of the light wandering in the garden. 'I loved playing here better than anywhere else,' he remembered. 'This was a wonderful place for gangs of bandits. I used to get the boys from the village in and we created mayhem.'

She smiled. 'I wonder how Baptista felt about that in her flower garden.'

'She didn't mind. She said what mattered was that there should be happiness here.' They had reached the rose arbour and sat on the wooden seat. 'I used to come out in the evening and find her sitting in this spot, with her eyes closed.'

'Did you ever find out why?' she asked cautiously.

'You mean did I know about Federico? Yes, the head gardener told me. He'd worked here for years and knew all about it. Apparently there were a lot of rumours when the young man vanished so suddenly.'

'That was the hardest for Baptista to bear,' Heather said. 'Not knowing. You surely don't think—?'

'I doubt it, but I have to admit that my grandfather was a man who wouldn't tolerate opposition.'

They had supper in the library, close to the open French windows. Renato's mood had mellowed and he went on reminiscing about the villa as he'd known it in his childhood.

'I always knew it had a special place in my mother's heart. Perhaps that's why it became enchanted to me too. The Residenza was just a building, but Bella Rosaria was special.'

'Then take it back.'

He gave her an ironic look. 'There's only one way I can do that.'

'No marriage,' she said at once. 'We both agreed.'

He shrugged. 'My mother is a very persuasive woman, and I'm a man with a strong sense of duty.'

She rested her elbows on the table and met his eyes. 'Rubbish!' she said firmly. 'I don't know what game you're playing, but you can forget it. No marriage. Not now. Not ever. You can take that as final.'

He grinned. 'Suppose I don't choose to?'

'Oh, stop this! I know you're only fooling but it's not fair to give the village ideas. Do you think I don't know why they were out in force, watching us? And the priest, practically giving us his blessing. You ought to stop them thinking things. It's not fair.'

'To whom?'

'To them. They obviously like the idea.'

'Yes, you've made yourself popular. And the fact that you know about sheep will be all over the district tonight. Everyone around here sees the propriety of our marriage as clearly as Mamma does.'

She laughed. 'They'd think differently if they could have heard what you said about swimming the Straits of Messina in lead weights.'

He winced. 'I deny it. I never said any such thing. Anyway, a man can grow wiser.'

She refused to rise to the bait. 'I'm going to bed,' she said.

'You're right. We'll make an early start in the morning. Don't be late. I dislike women who keep me waiting.'

This was so clearly meant to be provocative that she said, 'I really will kick your shins in a minute,' in a teasing voice.

'Exactly what Mamma advised, night and morning. You see, we're acting like an old married couple already.'

She began to laugh. She couldn't help it. She ought to at least try to stay cross with him, but the excellent wine and the company of a man who, for all his infuriating behaviour, was still more mysteriously attractive than anyone she'd ever known, was a potent combination. Tonight he'd been pleasant company, making her like him better than at any time before.

'That's better than the last time I heard you laugh,' he said approvingly.

The night in the garden, when she'd laughed on the edge of sobs, and he'd kissed her with a tenderness that had haunted her dreams since. She met his eyes and looked quickly away, confused. She no longer knew what she wanted.

They climbed the stairs together. Outside her door he took her hand, said gently, 'Goodnight, Heather,' and went across the corridor to his own room without waiting for her answer.

When she'd closed her door she stood for a long time, listening to the sound of her own heart beating. He would come to her tonight. She knew that beyond any doubt. Suddenly decided, she turned the key in her lock.

She undressed slowly, torn this way and that, until she crept to the door and unlocked it. Then she got into bed and lay listening to the creaks of the old house, as the night grew quiet around them, staring into the darkness.

Renato wanted to marry her. Or rather, he'd decided in favour of the marriage. That was more accurate. The family needed an heir, and Lorenzo had proved too unreliable, so Renato had reluctantly bowed his neck to the yoke. Marrying her would please his mother and satisfy his sense of duty.

Nothing else?

Yes. She'd challenged him, laughed at him, snubbed him. His pride was at stake. And he wanted to sleep with her. He'd made no bones about it. But she already knew how little physical relationships counted with him. When he'd soothed his pride and gained what he wanted—what then?

Hell is love without desire, and desire without love—desire without love—

At last she fell asleep.

CHAPTER NINE

WHEN they met at breakfast her mood was cool. Naturally she was glad of Renato's restraint the night before. If he'd tried to come to her bed it would have clouded the issue and she would have been angry at his calculation.

But the apparently easy way he'd resisted her was also a kind of calculation, and of the two it was the more insulting. She blushed to recall that she'd left her door unlocked, and he hadn't even tried it. One small victory to him. If she weakened he would control the situation, and that she mustn't allow.

He didn't seem to notice her reserve. His own mood was edgy. Over breakfast he spoke tersely, smiled very little and looked haggard.

The horses were brought round. Soon after they set out she realised that Renato had been right when he'd said the story of the sheep would be all over the district. Wherever they went she found none of the suspicion or hostility that she would have expected, considering that she was a stranger and a foreigner. By some mysterious bush telegraph they knew Renato had chosen her for his wife, they regarded the match as settled, and they approved.

Before long the beauty of the day had its effect on both of them, softening her mood and making him less tense. They stopped at a farm and sat in the sun, drinking rough home-made wine and eating goat's-milk cheese. Heather had been enchanted by Sicily from the first moment. Now she found new things to delight her wherever she looked.

'I love that,' she said, pointing to the ruins of a Greek

temple in the distance, with sheep and goats munching contentedly nearby. 'A great, ancient civilisation, side by side with everyday reality. The sheep aren't awed by the temple, and the temple isn't less splendid because of the sheep.'

He nodded agreement. 'It was built in honour of Ceres, the goddess of fertility and abundance. The more sheep the better.'

'And seeing them in harmony like that sums up so much about this country.'

'Do you know how like a Sicilian you sound?' he said. 'Talking as though this was a separate country, instead of part of Italy. We all do that.'

'Yes, I'd noticed. And it's more than a separate country. It's a separate world. There's nothing like it anywhere else.'

'And will you leave it? Turn your back on the welcome it's given you?'

'You're a very clever man.' She sighed. 'You've simply gone over my head again. Your mother has decided, the tenants have decided, Father Torrino tells me how much it will cost to repair the church roof—all because you've let them think it's a done deal. It makes me feel like the last piece in a jigsaw puzzle.'

'That's a very good analogy,' he said, tactfully bypassing her accusations. 'This is a jigsaw puzzle, with all the pieces fitting perfectly. You come into our lives from another country. You have different values, a different language, and yet there's a space waiting for you that's exactly your shape. The differences you bring will only enrich us. We can all see it. Why can't you?'

'Maybe because you come as part of the package,' she said darkly.

He gave her the vivid grin that could so powerfully disconcert her. 'Be brave. I'm not really so bad.'

'You are.'

'I'm not.'

'You are.'

They laughed at the same moment. It was pleasant to be sitting in the bright day, squabbling light-heartedly. In another moment she might have yielded. But then some perverse imp made her ask, 'Why did you change your mind? A couple of weeks ago nothing would make you consider it.'

'Mamma gave me a stern talking-to, and as I'm afraid of her I gave in.' He added outrageously, 'But very reluctantly.'

'Oh, stop it. I'm trying to be serious.'

'Then let's be serious. Arranged marriages can work very well when neither party is burdened with extravagant expectations. We've both seen the dangers of that, haven't we?'

'If you put it like that,' she said with a sigh, 'I suppose we have.'

'Shall we call it a bargain? Come, say yes so that I can call Mamma.'

'I suppose she's sitting by the phone, waiting to hear my answer?'

'Possibly, although I think she knew it was virtually decided.'

She frowned. 'Decided? Now wait a minute. No way was it decided.'

He made a hasty gesture. 'I put that badly. It's just that I told her I thought that when you and I had talked about it calmly—'

'What you told her,' Heather breathed, her eyes kindling, 'was that I was bound to give in. ''Just give me a few hours to talk some sense into her, Mamma, and you can start sending out the invitations.'' It was bad enough that you fooled people around here, but how dare you tell your mother it was settled?'

She got hastily to her feet.

Renato swore and rose too. 'Heather, will you listen to reason?'

'No, because I don't like your kind of reason. You pulled my strings to marry me to Lorenzo, only he wasn't there. Now you think you're going to pull my strings again—only, this time, *I* won't be there. Somebody ought to put you in a cage and charge admission, because you come right out of the ark. And you're the last man I could ever marry.'

A look of stubbornness settled on his face. 'But I've given her my word.'

'And *my* word is no.'

'This is Sicily, where a woman's word counts for nothing beside a man's.'

'Well, maybe I'm not as much a Sicilian as we all thought.'

'Why can't you face the inevitable?'

'Because I don't think it *is* inevitable. I'm meant for a better fate than to save you from the results of your own pride. Go back to your light affairs, Renato. Pay them, and forget them. That's all you're good for.'

His sharp intake of breath told him she'd flicked him on the raw. She stormed away to where the horses were tethered. The farmer was there and he smiled at her in a way she was coming to recognise. The sight only increased her sense of being trapped. She thanked him for his hospitality before jumping on her horse and galloping away.

Faster and faster she urged the willing animal, as

though she could outrun all the furies that pursued her whenever Renato Martelli was around. She could hear him behind her now, galloping hard to catch up, shouting something.

She couldn't make out the words, and she missed the signs that would have warned her what was about to happen: the sudden drop in temperature, the darkening of the sky. The first crack of thunder took her by surprise. Her horse was alarmed, missed his footing, found it again and managed to go on. But he'd lost speed, and in the need to control him she'd taken her eyes off Renato. Next thing he'd caught up with her.

'Go on to the temple,' he cried. 'It's nearer than the farm.'

Before she could reply there was another crack of thunder and the heavens opened. She gasped. This wasn't rain as she knew it. It was a flood, a torrent that crashed onto her all at once, pounding like hammers, drenching her in the first second.

'Come on!' he yelled.

She could no longer see the temple in the downpour, and found it only by following him. It loomed suddenly out of the wall of rain, no longer cheerful as in the sun, but almost sinister.

'There,' he cried, pointing to the far end. 'There's some cover.'

But the cover turned out to be too small. There was only just room for the horses, so they put the distressed animals inside, and endured the downpour themselves.

'Damn!' he yelled. 'I thought we had another day at least.'

But now she'd got her second wind Heather was feeling good. The noise of the water, the thunder, the fierceness of the rain against her body, was exhilarating. Renato stared at her, realising that this wasn't the woman he knew, but a new one who revelled in the violence of the elements. She turned and stared back at him, laughing, challenging. The next moment he'd pulled her into his arms.

It felt good to be kissed by a man whose control was slipping, who wanted her almost against his will. There was a driving purpose in his lips that thrilled her. He kissed her mouth, her nose, her eyes, seeking her feverishly as though nothing was ever enough. She gasped and clung to him. The rain had soaked through the thin material of their shirts, making them almost vanish. She relished in the feel of his body, the muscular shape of his arms and shoulders, the heavy bull neck, the sheer primitive force of the man. This was what she'd craved even while she was fending him off, because, like him, she needed her own terms.

But what was happening between them was on nobody's terms: need, craving, curiosity, antagonism. They were all there, mixed up with a desire that obeyed no laws but its own. Her heart was pounding so wildly that he felt it and laid his hand between her breasts.

'Could Lorenzo make you feel like this?' he demanded. 'Can't you feel the difference?'

'There's no difference,' she cried. 'You and Lorenzo are two of a kind. Both selfish, careless of other people's feelings, thinking of women as creatures to be used.'

She wondered what perversity made her hold out against a man who was gaining such a strong hold on her heart and senses. But ancient, wise instinct warned her not to let Renato have too easy a victory. She didn't know what their future would hold, whether it might be love or just desire. But it would be built on what was happening now, and if she didn't stand her ground she would always regret it.

But he too seemed to understand this, because he was making it so hard for her to hold out, caressing her with his lips that murmured seductively of passion and pleasure, passion so intense that it was destiny, pleasure too great to be resisted.

Hell is desire without love.

They shared desire but no love, and a marriage based on that faulty basis could only end in bitterness. She must cling to that, but it was hard when her body clamoured as never before for what only this man could give.

As abruptly as it had started, the rain eased off to a light drizzle. She broke free and turned away from him, but that helped her not at all. Wherever she looked she saw the carvings and statues depicting Ceres and the fertility she demanded. Here was corn, ripe for harvest, there were animals mating vigorously on a frieze that ran all around above their heads. And everywhere were men and women united in a fury of ecstatic creation.

Ceres was a ruthless goddess, sworn to make the little people she ruled fruitful, at any cost. To tempt them she dangled the sweetness of desire, but when her purpose was achieved the desire turned to ashes.

Renato came up behind her. He'd followed her gaze and understood everything she was thinking. 'There's no fighting it,' he said. 'Certainly not in this place, which was built to remind us how helpless we are in the hands of the gods.'

'Do you believe that?'

'I believe there are some forces we can't withstand.'

'And what do you think the gods meant for us?' she asked, turning on him.

'I'll tell you what they didn't mean. They didn't mean

for us to live peacefully. You and I could never do that. There's something in you that drives me crazy, and there's something in me that brings out a temper you never show to anyone else. We've fought from the moment we met, and we'll probably fight until the last moment of our lives. But we'll pass those lives together because *I will not let you marry any other man.*'

Looking into his face, she was swept by a wild mood. It was the same as the one that she'd known on the jet ski when she had incited him to ride on out of sight of the boat. It had almost cost her her life then, and now it might decide the rest of her life.

'Do you understand?' he said. 'Answer me.'

She answered, not in words, but in a slow smile that made him growl and pull her hard against him. 'Are you tormenting me for the pleasure of it?'

'What do you think?' she asked, speaking quietly so that he couldn't hear, had to make out the movement of her lips.

'I think I won't let you torment me any more,' he growled.

She laughed recklessly. 'How will you stop me?'

'Don't challenge me, Heather. You'll lose.'

'I think I've already won.'

She'd won his lips crushing hers, one arm tight around her waist, the other behind her neck, so that she couldn't have escaped if she'd wanted to. But she didn't want to. She wanted to stay in his arms and enjoy her prize to the full. Because afterwards would come the day of reckoning, when she would discover what else she had won with this strange, mysterious, complicated man.

'Tell me that you never slept with him,' he said hoarsely.

'If I did, I had every right to. I was his, not yours.'

'Tell me you didn't.'

'It doesn't concern you. You don't own me. You never will.'

He stepped back from her. He was trembling as though he'd run a long race.

'I do,' he said. 'And I always will.'

He fell silent. He might have been waiting for her response, but she was determined to say nothing. Slowly the stormy look died out of his eyes, leaving bleakness behind. 'The rain has stopped,' he said. 'We should leave before it starts again.'

At the villa he stayed only long enough to dry off and change into some of the dry clothes that were still in his room. Heather went to her own room to change, and when she emerged Renato had already gone.

'He said to say goodbye,' Jocasta explained. 'But he couldn't stay.'

'No, I didn't think he would.'

She ate alone that evening, and picked so delicately at the food that Jocasta privately berated her husband, demanding to know if he wanted to drive the mistress away by his bad cooking.

She was late going to bed. As the moon came up she wandered in the garden, finding her way easily along silvered paths. The rose bush shone in the cool light, symbol of a love that had never really died.

That was what she'd thought awaited her here: the sweetness and tenderness of love. It was the kind of gentle experience that, as a northerner, she had instinctively understood.

Instead, in this country of fierce sun and fiercer rain, she'd found a passion as primitive as time itself, passion as these varied, unpredictable people understood it, and it had revealed that at heart she was one of them.

Very well. If she was to be a Sicilian, then she would meet the problem not merely with Sicilian intensity, but with Sicilian cunning.

She was swept again by the memory of Renato's lips on hers, the way he'd pulled her against him so that her body moulded itself against his. These things had made her want to cry *Yes* with every part of her.

But his mouth had spoken the language of pride and possession, and no woman of spirit could consent to that. So her words had denied him while her senses clamoured for him. It seemed there was no way to solve the riddle.

Unless....

Next day she drove down to the Residenza in the late afternoon, and found Baptista fresh from her nap, bright-eyed and cheerful. They had tea and cakes together on the terrace as the afternoon light faded. The rains had left everywhere looking freshly washed, and now that the hottest part of summer had gone this time of day was cool and pleasant. Encouraged by Baptista, she described how she was spending her time at the villa.

'The local priest paid me a ceremonial visit, and said very anxiously that he hoped I played chess. I assured him that I did, and he went away happy.'

Baptista chuckled. 'Father Torrino is a dear man but the worst chess player in the world. You'll have to let him win sometimes. So you're fitting into the community. That's excellent.'

'Oh, they're all looking me up and down and wondering if I'll "do",' Heather said with a smile. 'They seem to think that I will. It's a happy place. No wonder you love it.' After a moment she added significantly, 'I really don't want to leave.'

'I was sure you wouldn't.'

'But it's not that easy.' Heather sipped her tea and thought for a moment before asking, 'How many men did you turn down before you finally said yes?'

'Five or six. My poor parents were tearing their hair, but they persevered.'

Out of the corner of her eye Heather became aware of a shadow on the curtain, and then the figure of a man appearing. She was sure Baptista also knew he was there, but neither of them took the slightest notice of him. Nor did he speak. He was listening intently.

'It's not just the man who has to be right,' Baptista continued, 'but the circumstances. That's one advantage of using an intermediary. You negotiate the important decisions first, and then there's less to quarrel about.'

'Oh, I don't know,' Heather murmured, still refusing to acknowledge Renato's presence, although he'd poured himself some tea, and taken a seat a little behind them. 'With certain people there would always be something to quarrel about because they're just naturally annoying.'

'I totally agree. A good intermediary takes that into account. Some men are harder to match than others on account of being—how shall I put it?'

'Full of themselves,' Heather supplied.

Baptista gave a delighted snort. 'I love your English idioms. So perfectly expressive. And you have another one—"where to get off!" Such a man needs a wife who can tell him where to get off. As for her, if perhaps she finds her life a little unfocused and lacking in direction, and if he can offer her a life that can remedy these problems—she might well decide to overlook his deficiencies.'

'There's another matter to be settled,' Heather pointed out. 'Fidelity. The party on my side wouldn't want to find herself standing in line behind Julia and Minetta and—'

'Never heard of them,' growled a masculine voice from behind.

'I think he'll decide to forget that he's ever heard of them,' Baptista observed blandly.

'Good,' Heather said. 'My party would expect things to stay that way. Did somebody speak?'

The voice growled again. *'Zoccu non fa pi tia ad autra non fari.'*

'We seem to have been joined by a spirit presence,' Baptista remarked, unperturbed. 'It has just reminded us of a Sicilian proverb: Do not do to others what you don't wish them to do to you.'

'The point is taken,' Heather observed gravely. 'Fidelity on both sides.'

'Excellent. There are certain other matters to be decided in advance. Like, where they are going to live. I refused two suitors because they disliked Bella Rosaria and wouldn't spend any time there. All I wanted was a few weeks in the summer, but they wouldn't budge.'

'A few weeks in summer sounds ideal,' Heather said.

'And the rest of the time here because he does so much business from this house.'

'Of course, he would need to remain at the heart of his business,' Heather agreed. 'But I expect you slipped away to the villa sometimes on your own?'

'Indeed I did. As I'm sure you would wish to do. Although I doubt you'd be on your own because he loves the place too, and might burden you with his company more often than you'd like.'

'I wouldn't mind. He's at his best at the villa.'

'Ah, you've discovered that.'

'Almost human. And it's nice to have something in common.'

'Once that has been decided,' Baptista resumed, 'all

that would remain would be to call in the lawyers and arrange the legal details. As to the dowry—'

'The bride offers Bella Rosaria, a very desirable estate,' Heather pointed out.

'An excellent dowry,' Baptista agreed, 'which will remain her property—'

'But I thought—that is, *she* thought she'd be giving it back to the Martelli family,' Heather protested.

'After the marriage she'll be part of the Martelli family,' Baptista pointed out. 'Besides, a woman is in a stronger position in Sicily if she has some property of her own. You should advise your party to take my word for it.'

Heather nodded. 'She will do so. In fact, she's very aware of how much she owes to your wisdom and judgement in bringing this difficult case to a successful conclusion. Have we forgotten anything?'

'I don't think so.'

'In that case,' Heather said with a sudden air of resolution, 'you can tell your party that my party finds the arrangements quite satisfactory.'

She rose. Baptista held out a hand and Heather helped her to stand. Then the two women went slowly into the house, leaving Renato alone in the gathering twilight, drinking his tea and staring moodily out to sea. Neither of them had spared him so much as a glance.

CHAPTER TEN

FOR her second wedding in Palermo Cathedral Heather chose a much simpler dress than her first. It was of ivory silk, because that suited her lightly tanned complexion better than white, and she borrowed it from a hire shop in Palermo.

'It didn't cost me a penny,' she told Renato and Baptista triumphantly. 'I made them a gift of the old one and they were delighted to let me hire one free.'

Baptista gave a crow of triumph. 'What a business-woman! Didn't I tell you?' This was to Renato.

'You did.' He was grinning. 'Perhaps your suggestion was right, Mamma.'

'Right?' Heather looked from one to the other.

'Mamma thinks you should join the business at once,' Renato explained.

'I shall be retiring soon and you must take my place,' Baptista said. 'Otherwise there won't be a female voice on the board, and that would be disaster.'

'You're on the board?'

'You'll enjoy our board meetings,' Renato told her ironically. 'First Mamma tells us what she wants. Then the meeting begins, she proposes the motion and we all vote according to her instructions.'

'Baloney!' Heather said frankly.

'No wonder Mamma wants you to take her place. You're as big a bully as she is.'

'Take her place?'

'I can't go on for ever,' Baptista said. 'My dear, you

have brains, beauty and business sense. In short, you're a considerable asset. Naturally I was determined to "acquire" you.'

It might have sounded clinical but Heather already knew that her future mother-in-law loved her. The effect, as Baptista had intended, was to make her feel valued, and to show her to herself not just as bride, but as a woman taking her place in a community. This was what arranged marriages were for.

She would have preferred a quiet wedding, but every guest from last time must be asked back, or they would be offended. So the preparations went ahead on the same scale. In the kitchens the chefs worked night and day to outdo their previous efforts. Even the cake had an extra tier.

There was one other aspect which would be exactly the same. Once more Bernardo would be the best man, and on the night before the wedding Heather drove to Palermo Airport to collect Angie, who had flown in to be her bridesmaid. They dined together in a restaurant, and slipped into the house later, unseen by Bernardo.

'He really hasn't suspected?' Angie asked as she prepared for bed in their old room.

'Not a thing. Nobody has mentioned your coming, and the first Bernardo will know is when he sees you walking down the aisle with me tomorrow. You haven't changed, have you?'

'Not by a whisper,' Angie said wistfully. 'And him?'

'He's as unhappy as you are,' Heather said. 'Trust me. I'm going to fix this.'

'Goodness, but you sounded like Baptista then,' Angie said, startled.

'That's what they want me for,' Heather said lightly.

'Pardon?'

'This is an arranged marriage. Very suitable.'

'And that's why you're marrying Renato? Because it's "suitable".'

'Certainly,' Heather said, a little stiffly.

Angie smiled. 'You're kidding yourself.'

The morning came. The family departed. Cousin Enrico, who was giving her away, escorted her to the car, and in a few minutes they'd reached the cathedral. This time there was no breeze to stir her veil, no crowd to cry *'grazziusu'*. No romance, no poetry. Only the certainty that this time her bridegroom would be there, waiting to make the deal. A sensible marriage for sensible people.

Then they had started the long journey down the aisle to the high altar. With a sense of shock she saw Renato's face. Not sensible. Not businesslike. Strangely pale, stunned, exactly as he'd looked on that other day as she descended the stairs to take his arm for him to lead her to her marriage with his brother.

She'd meant to glance at Bernardo to see how he reacted to Angie, but the sight of Renato, his eyes fixed on her with a look she couldn't understand, wiped everything else from her mind. The cathedral vanished, the guests disappeared. There was only herself and Renato, about to become a part of each other's lives for ever.

The whole congregation seemed to he holding its breath as they made their responses, and to heave a collective sigh when they turned to walk back down the aisle, into the sunlight: husband and wife. The arrangement was made, the deal done. Both parties were satisfied.

At the reception in the Residenza they each managed to get through their parts without too much self-consciousness. Heather smiled and cut the cake. They toasted each other in champagne and tried not to seem too aware of what everyone was thinking. There was applause as they took the dance floor together.

Out of the corner of her eye Heather saw Angie dancing with Bernardo. They seemed lost in each other, but their faces were distraught, almost desperate, and her heart sank.

'Did you really think it would work, bringing her here?' Renato murmured.

'I hoped,' she said wistfully. 'They love each other so much.'

'Which is why neither of them can see reason. Not like us.'

'I guess that makes us the lucky ones,' she said, smiling.

He returned her smile. 'I think we might be.'

Something in that smile made her aware of the movement of his legs against hers through the material of her bridal gown. His hand was firm in the small of her back, and he was holding her very close. Once before they had danced, and she'd fought to deny her growing physical awareness of him. But now she didn't have to deny it. Her heart beat a little faster.

At last the guests began to leave, except for the ones who were staying the night, and the bride and groom were free to slip away. Her things had already been moved into the room with the big four-poster bed that for years he had occupied alone.

Now it was hers too. Signora Martelli.

There was only one light in the room, a bedside lamp that cast a small glow over the deep red counterpane and the rest of the room into mysterious shadow. The long mirror showed her to herself, a faint muted figure, still uncertain whether she really belonged here.

Something in the silence made her turn quickly and see

Renato standing just inside the door. She hadn't heard him come in. How long, she wondered, had he been there, looking at her with that strange expression that she couldn't read?

In this light he looked taller and more imposing than ever, except that when he moved towards her there was a new hesitancy in his manner, and she realised that he wasn't really very sure of himself either.

Renato had had champagne set there on ice, to wait for them, with two tall crystal glasses. Renato poured two glasses and offered one to her. She raised it to him, feeling her heart quicken its beating beneath the white dress.

'To us,' he said. They clinked glasses.

She was still in full bridal regalia, but now he lifted off the pearl tiara and removed her veil himself, causing her hair to fall down about her shoulders. Abruptly she set her glass down. Her hand was shaking.

'Are you all right?' he asked. 'It must have been a great strain for you, going through today with all those faces staring at you, wondering.'

'For you too. In fact they were probably wondering more about you, how you felt taking on the woman your brother—ouch!'

'I'm sorry,' he said swiftly releasing her hair where his hand had suddenly tightened. 'I didn't mean to do that. I think we should agree never to refer to that—or to him—again. It's over. It didn't happen.'

Yes, she thought, that was the only way they could live—as though it hadn't happened.

When Renato spoke again it was in a suspiciously cheerful voice, as though he were forcing himself to change the subject.

'Did you see Enrico and Giuseppe vying for Mamma's favours today?'

'Yes. Poor Enrico was hopping with rage when she danced with Giuseppe. If she hadn't danced with him straight after I dread to think what would have happened.'

'Mamma wouldn't have done that,' he said lightly. 'It wouldn't have been proper, and today has been a day of great propriety. We should congratulate ourselves. We've made a wise marriage, bearing in mind the interests of our family and community. This is what sensible people do.'

'It's an excellent business arrangement,' she agreed. 'We both gain.'

'I'm glad you see the position so clearly.'

But as he spoke he was letting his fingertips rest against her neck, setting off a soft excitement deep within her that made a mockery of his prosaic words. She met his eyes, wondering why there was a frown far back in them.

'You haven't changed your mind?' he asked abruptly.

'No, I haven't changed my mind.'

'Ah, yes, you're a woman of your word, I remember.' He drew her close, looking intently into her face as though trying to divine something she hadn't told him.

She had the feeling that he couldn't find it, because the little frown between his eyes didn't abate. If anything it was more intense as he lowered his head so that his lips could touch her neck. She cupped his head instinctively, feeling how well it fitted there.

As his mouth moved persuasively over her skin his fingers were working on the fastening at the back of her dress. It whispered to the ground and she felt the cool night air against her skin.

But she herself couldn't be cool. She was already burning with need for him. Something that had started the day he walked into the department store and challenged her was about to come to fruition, and she would find whether she'd gambled everything on a false dream.

He tossed his jacket and shirt aside and took her into his arms. His kiss was gentle, almost everything held back until they knew each other a little better. Their other kisses had been fierce, antagonistic. Tonight, for the first time, they had time to kiss in peace, giving each other the benefit of leisurely exploration, no rush, no quarrelling, just a man and a woman free to think only of each other.

She tried not to think of all the other, cynical kisses his lips had bestowed, or she would grow too jealous. She wanted him all to herself, now and for ever. Her mouth told him so as she welcomed him inside, relishing the feel of his tongue exploring her, teasing and inciting her. His mouth was warm and persuasive, cajoling her into pleasure. She answered with her own lips and tongue, with movements she hadn't even known she knew, but which seemed to please him because he gave a little growl of pleasure and redoubled his onslaught.

She didn't know where her flimsy slip went, or how she came to be lying on the bed while he tossed aside the rest of his clothes and joined her, pulling her into his arms so that she felt his chest against her, as smooth as the marble of the statues that dotted this ancient island. He was part of it, part of a civilisation that went back almost to the dawn of time, but what she sensed in him now was timeless. Civilisations had arisen from it, yet it was uncivilised, primitive and thrilling.

Once before he'd seen her naked, but she hadn't known. Now she was in his arms again, and this time he was as naked as she, pressing her against his hard body while his hands roved over her. She explored him in turn, tentatively at first, then with growing confidence as she discovered how excitingly masculine he felt against her palms, the tautness of his muscles like sprung steel.

At some point he switched out the bedside lamp so that they were almost in darkness. Only a little light came from the great curtain-hung windows. It might have been any man holding her against him, caressing her body intimately with such skilful hands. But then she sensed the power tempered by gentleness in his embrace, felt the hard, muscular length of his thighs against her own, and knew that this could be no other man but Renato.

She felt his touch along the length of her inner thigh, seeking and finding the heart of her. Shockwaves of desire went through her as she waited for him. In the dim light she could see the gleam of his eyes. She thought they seemed troubled, almost hesitant.

'Renato…' she breathed.

'You're sure—tell me that you're sure—'

It was hard to speak through the tide of warmth engulfing her but she managed to whisper, 'I'm sure—I want you—'

The next moment the world was transformed into a different place as he slowly entered her, and she became his. But she had always been his. If she'd doubted it before she knew it now. She held him tightly, feeling the pleasure mount high and then higher until the world dissolved. Then she was nothing, only heat and darkness and whispered words that she didn't understand, except that they came from the man who had become one with her and made her one with him.

When it was over he didn't release her, but held on as though he was afraid she would slip away. But she didn't want to slip away. She wanted to stay here for ever. She fell easily into a sweet sleep, but awoke an hour later to find him watching her. He smiled and cradled her until she slept again. The last thought in her mind was the memory of his eyes, brooding, watching, never letting her go.

It was too late in the year for a honeymoon on the boat, so they went to the airport the next morning. Angie came with them. Bernardo was still implacable and she was going home. They saw her off to England before catching the flight to Rome. After that they were going on to Paris. It was partly a working trip, as they visited their biggest customers, but Heather enjoyed becoming part of the business. In Paris they toured the couturiers and she acquired a new wardrobe that she wore for entertaining Renato's customers in the evenings. French was one of the languages she'd studied, hoping to rise in Gossways, and she spoke it well enough to get by.

'I shall start getting suspicious,' Renato said as they got undressed in their suite at the Hyatt Regency. 'I keep getting too many compliments about *la belle Madame Martelli, très chic, très merveilleuse.*'

'I'm just trying to do you credit.'

'Hm!' His tone was deeply cynical and she chuckled. He was helping her off with a little black number she'd worn for the first time that night, but something provocative in her laugh made his hands move faster, more determinedly. The next moment the little black dress was lying in ruins on the floor and she was in his arms.

'Renato—'

'Shut up, I'll buy you another,' was the last thing he said before he silenced both of them. And in a few seconds the movement of his lips and hands had driven all else from her mind.

After their first lovemaking she had slipped easily into the rhythm of passion, so that she found herself wanting him at all times, day or night. At first her own eagerness embarrassed her slightly, but that soon passed, and with every day she learned something new about physical love.

She knew that she pleased him as much as he pleased her because nothing was too good for her. He rarely spoke of feelings, never his own. Nor did he often say a word to her that opened doors into his mind. But she had only to express a wish to have it granted.

Once he said a strange thing. As she sat looking at yet another gift of jewellery, he said abruptly, 'You think I overdo it, don't you?'

Thinking only to tease him she joked, 'Not at all. After all, you did once offer me twenty thousand to sleep with you.'

But she regretted it when she saw his brows snap. Renato wasn't without a sense of humour, but he found it hard to laugh at himself. He didn't vent his displeasure on her, but he grew quiet in a way she was learning meant that he was upset. And when she said, 'I was only teasing,' he brightened too quickly.

'Of course,' he said. 'I'm just in a strange mood. Where shall we eat?'

After which the subject was closed, despite all her efforts to raise it and put things right. Nor did she ever wear the jewellery because every time she tried he found fault with her appearance, until it had to be abandoned.

Jewellery was the least of it. Soon after they returned to Sicily she happened to mention the day she'd arrived, when he'd told her Lorenzo was soon flying to New York.

'I was going to turn my pea shooter onto you, but then you said I was going too, so I had to put my pea shooter away.'

'You fancied New York?'

'I'll say. That's one of the really annoying things about you—'

'Among so many—'

'Definitely—the way you take the wind out of my sails when I'm getting good and mad at you.'

They were in bed, relaxing after making love. He grinned at her, curled up in the crook of his arm. 'You enjoy getting mad at me, don't you?'

'It's one of my more enjoyable hobbies, yes.'

'Go on looking at me out of those glittering eyes. It gives me pleasurable thoughts and makes all the effort of landing you worth it.'

'Landing me? I'm not a fish.'

'But you were a challenge.'

'Yes, I know some of the devious methods you used. You were supposed to be persuading Gossways to take me back on the programme, but you never called them.'

Something in his silence told her the monstrous truth. 'It's worse than that, isn't it?' she demanded, sitting up sharply. 'You called some buddy among the big shots and made him promise *not* to have me back.'

'I admit nothing.'

'You don't need to....'

'You've got smoke coming out of your ears again.' He sat up and reached for her. 'Very pretty smoke, mind you....' The last words were muffled as she thumped him with a pillow hard enough to send him right off the bed. He grabbed her as he went, and they ended up on the floor together.

'I thought if I could make you mad enough with me—' he tried to explain as he grappled with her wriggling body '—you'd marry me just for the pleasure of—in my mother's charming phrase—kicking my shins every day. Ouch!'

'Oh, stop making a fuss. I only used my bare foot.'

She managed to get free and climb back onto the bed, but he followed her, pinning her down. She looked up at his face, furious, her breasts rising and falling. 'I'm warning you Renato, I'm good 'n' mad.'

'I know. I've just got a fresh bruise to prove it.'

'Let go of me.'

'When we've had a talk about this—' His eyes roved over her nakedness, and his speech slowed as though something had distracted him. 'It's—important to talk,' he said at last. 'That's what—' his gaze seemed riveted by the sight of her nipples, rosy and expectant '—that's what—good marriages—are made of—'

'Talking?' she said breathlessly.

'Confidence between—' his fingertips brushed one nipple '—husband and wife—trust—where was I?'

'Trust—' she gasped.

'Trust—and shared values—honour—'

'Honour? You? The most devious, conniving, manipulative— *Don't stop!*'

'I wasn't going to,' he whispered against her skin, continuing the work that had driven her half wild. After that there were no more words, no thoughts, just sensations, need and blinding nothingness. The end was explosive enough to blot out the world, leaving only heat and swirling darkness, and somewhere a man with strong arms and powerful loins to bring her joy.

In a sense that was just the trouble. There was joy, bliss, ecstasy, but not precisely happiness. Not unhappiness either, for how could any bride be unhappy with a husband who gave her all his attention and took her to new lands of sensation she'd never dreamed of before? But not to be unhappy wasn't the same as being happy. Especially when she realised that sometimes he would use their sexual harmony to distract her from subjects he wanted to avoid.

She never gave their conversation another thought until a week later he put the tickets for New York into her hands.

'What's this?' she gasped.

'Call it a second honeymoon.'

'But we've barely got back from our first.'

He shrugged. 'I have business in New York. Of course, if you don't want to come—' He reached for the tickets but she seized them and backed away, laughing.

They were in New York for a week, and although he looked in on the odd customer, it never seemed to Heather that this was a vital part of his schedule. She wondered if he'd done it only to please her, but while he murmured many passionate words when they were alone in the night, he never spoke a tender, loving word by day, and his manner, although pleasant, didn't invite her close. Sometimes it was like living with two men.

When they returned home she became more involved in the running of Bella Rosaria. She was wise enough to let Luigi keep the reins in his experienced hands, but subject to his advice she visited her tenants, discussed their problems, and began to make decisions. The revenues that came in were her own. Renato refused to make any claim on them, and even insisted on giving her a wife's allowance. She would have liked to refuse but didn't because she suspected that he would be hurt. It was no more than a suspicion, because she had to guess his feelings, but she sensed that she'd got this one right.

Because of his reticence she couldn't speak out about her fast growing feelings for him. She guessed that it had been growing for some time, but she only discovered its strength when he had to be away for a week. She wouldn't have thought it possible to miss one person so much. It wasn't just her senses that longed for Renato, but her heart craved him night and day. It was their first separation since their marriage and it was almost unbearable.

It was nothing like the gentle pleasure of loving Lorenzo, which now looked more like a feeble infatuation with every day that passed. This love was savage and all-powerful, wiping out lesser feelings, leaving her helpless and desperate.

Their reunion was overwhelming, and somehow she was sure she would find the moment to hint at her feelings and hear something about his own. But his most enthusiastic talk was of deals he had done, and there was something in his cheerfulness that kept her at a distance.

CHAPTER ELEVEN

As with any properly conducted business arrangement the terms of their marriage were adhered to on both sides. Renato had promised Heather a place in the firm, and one day she came home from shopping to find him regarding her with a teasing look.

'How would you like to take a trip for the firm?' he asked. 'I need someone to fix up some deals in Scotland.'

'But isn't that Lorenzo's territory? In fact he's in England right now—'

'He's got some unexpected problems that are going to keep him there,' Renato broke in hastily. 'If you take over Scotland it will ease the pressure on him.'

She was ambitious for the chance. Even so, her first thought had been, I'll have to be away from him. But Renato seemed delighted at the thought of her going.

Next day she was on a flight to Edinburgh. She booked into a newly opened luxury hotel on Princes Street, and spent the next few days selling Martelli produce all over the most exclusive parts of the city, including the hotel itself. Her trip was a triumphant success, but it was spoiled for her by a persistent ache of loneliness that wouldn't go away.

On the last day she called home just to hear his voice, but he was out and wouldn't be back that day. The violence of her disappointment almost winded her. She pulled herself together and went out to work, forcing herself to concentrate, and ending up with a full order book that she was eager to show Renato.

But she saw him a lot sooner than she expected.

Returning to the hotel, she was pulled up short by the sight of Renato and the manager sitting together in the bar. Her first reaction was stunned delight. They rose to greet her, all smiles, and her husband complimented her on the deal she'd done with the hotel.

'Your wife is a true Martelli, Renato,' the manager said. 'She drives a hard bargain.'

'And not only here,' Renato agreed. 'All over town, apparently.'

So that was it. Her brief hope that he'd been missing her died stillborn. He was here as a businessman, finding out the skills of his newest sales rep, 'all over town'.

While the manager was ordering drinks, Renato looked at her glowering face and observed, 'I'd hoped you'd be more pleased to see me.'

'I don't like being checked up on,' she muttered.

He seemed disconcerted, then pulled himself together. 'It's not exactly that—'

'I think it is,' she said with a sigh. 'I don't blame you, but let's drop it.'

No more was said. In the evening they were the manager's guests for dinner, and the two men toasted her. That night in their suite she displayed her order book and received her husband's wholehearted praise. She tried to look behind his eyes, but he wouldn't let her, and when he embraced her, smiling, and said, 'Let me show you just how pleased with you I am,' she stopped worrying about anything else but the delight to be found in his arms.

They stayed another two days, while she finalised her deals. He made a few suggestions but otherwise didn't interfere. On the last night they celebrated over a meal which they had served in their bedroom, 'for the sake of convenience,' as they both delicately put it. And when the time came they were glad there were only a few steps to travel.

As they lay languorously entwined in each other's arms afterwards he murmured, 'You're not really annoyed that I came here, are you?'

'I thought you had important business to see to?'

'What could be more important?'

'Ah, yes, I might have been losing money hand over fist, mightn't I?'

'You forget, I first met you as a demon saleswoman,' he reminded her lightly.

But this sparring wasn't enough for her. Surely now, when they lay so close, she could nudge him towards greater frankness?

'But what do we really know about each other?' she asked. 'In bed, a good deal. Outside, very little.'

'Nonsense. You know a lot about me. Devious, conniving, manipulative—I forget the other words you used but it sounds as though you know me very well. Besides—' he became serious, '—in bed a man and a woman find their greatest truth.'

'Yes,' she said wistfully, 'but not their only truth.'

'How much do you think the other truths matter?'

'Not much now, maybe. But later—as the years pass—'

'Leave the years to take care of themselves,' he said easily.

She made a cynical sound that would have been a snort if she hadn't been a lady. 'That from you—the man who has to plan everything years ahead.'

He didn't say anything for a while, but at last he asked in a strange voice, 'Are we talking about Lorenzo? I'd rather not, but if so, then yes, I admit it. I try to plan too much. Your marriage to him would have been a mistake.

I knew that the day we went out on the boat, but it was too late. What could I do? Seduce my brother's fiancée?'

'*Try* to seduce her,' she said firmly. 'Don't take it for granted that you'd have succeeded.'

He grunted. 'What would you like to bet against my chances?'

She thought of the sensations that had almost drowned her as he rubbed oil into her back. But more than that was the moment of tender understanding between them as she held his wrist and looked at the scar. No passion then. Just an alarmed awareness of each other as people with thoughts and feelings.

'Well?' he persisted. 'If I'd forgotten my honour that day, would you have forgotten yours?'

'It was different. I was in love with Lorenzo.'

'Love is a complication,' he agreed. 'Even when it's an illusion.'

She longed to remind him of his own words about love—'I believed in things I don't believe in now'—and ask if he still meant them. Surely their closeness must have made him feel differently? But her courage failed at the last moment.

'I guess we'll never know the truth,' she said lightly.

'Probably not. But I knew how badly I wanted you, and I kept my distance. When Lorenzo took flight I was secretly glad, except that after that you hated me. I couldn't blame you, but there seemed no way of approaching you.'

'If Mamma hadn't decided to arrange a marriage between us, would you have let me go away?'

'No,' he said simply. 'I wanted you.'

Wanted, she noted. Not loved.

'But when we talked you became angry,' he continued. 'She was the only one you would listen to.'

'You mean—you were behind it?'

'I knew what was in her mind. I could have discouraged her. I didn't.'

'But you hit the roof at the idea of marrying me.'

'Only after you roared with laughter. What did you expect me to say after that?'

She stared at him. It was on the tip of her tongue to demand, But why didn't you just *ask* me to marry you?

But she couldn't say it. It would reveal too much about her emotions, and she was safer not doing that with a man who kept his own emotions hidden.

And that, of course, was the answer. Renato wouldn't risk asking because it meant revealing himself. So he'd sought to negotiate a deal at arm's length.

Now she remembered something else he'd said. 'I would invite betrayal by expecting it.'

Not betrayal. She could never betray him. But withdrawal. A man who kept his heart hidden made it impossible for her to do anything else.

'So Mamma was acting as your emissary?' she asked lightly.

'After the way you'd been hurt, an impersonal approach seemed wiser.'

It was all so reasonable. She wanted to scream at how reasonable it was. Or maybe she just wanted to scream that he had so little to offer.

Baptista was her tower of strength. After the marriage she had never relinquished her role as intermediary.

'That's what I call it,' she observed one day as they sat together at Bella Rosaria, watching the rain. 'Some people would call it being an interfering mother-in-law.'

Heather smiled and squeezed her hand. 'You know better than that.'

'Before you there was no woman who could make him

stop and think, force him to forget his arrogance, and learn to trust and love again. So I "acquired" you because he needed you so much. But was I being selfish to you?'

'No, Mamma. We're very happy in many ways. And sometimes I can feel him wanting to reach out to me, but he always pulls back. How can I ever tell him that I love him?'

'Must it be told in words?'

'For me it must.'

'I think his feelings for you were coming alive since before your first "wedding". *Maria vergine*, how lucky we all were that Lorenzo had the good sense to abort it!'

'Lorenzo?' Heather echoed with a chuckle. 'Good sense?'

'He saw what needed doing to avert disaster, and he did it. How miserable you'd all be now if he hadn't! He's still rather irresponsible. But he's developing into an excellent and *sensible* young man.' She added with a twinkle, 'But don't tell him I said that.'

'I won't. Besides, if he became too sensible he wouldn't be Lorenzo. Now, Renato is all good sense. It's his driving force. He doesn't love me because he doesn't understand love. He understands need and want and acquisition. But he knows nothing about the heart.'

'You are mistaken,' her mother-in-law said firmly. 'He simply hasn't yet discovered that you matter to him more than anything else in the world. That will take time. Perhaps years.'

Heather said nothing, but in her heart she wondered if she could spend years waiting for what might never happen. She saw Baptista watching her, and knew that she wondered too.

* * *

Winter was passing, the rains eased off, leaving the soil rich and black for the spring sowing. Everywhere there was a sense of life renewing. Her first spring. Her first lambing. The harvest that was gathered in this year would be truly her harvest.

She was managing the estate well. Everyone said so, even Luigi, who really did the work of managing it.

'You at least can't be fooled,' she chided him.

'No fooling. You do well. You stand back and let me do my job. That's clever.'

Her revenues were excellent. She spent as Luigi advised, otherwise practised thrift, and built up such excellent credit with the bank that she was able to assist Renato through a minor cashflow problem. There was pleasure in that, but it was lessened by his insistence on paying her a proper rate of interest, 'to keep the books straight'. It was an entirely reasonable explanation, and she couldn't find the words to explain her irrational sadness.

These days she saw little of Lorenzo, whose job occupied him abroad almost permanently. His next visit to England coincided with Renato's departure to spend ten days in Rome. Renato didn't suggest that Heather should go with him.

She spent a couple of days at Bella Rosaria and returned to the Residenza to find that Baptista was out visiting friends, and not expected back until late. In her room she unpacked, trying to ignore the feeling of restlessness that had seized her. She chided herself for being ungrateful. She had everything—almost everything that she could want. But it seemed that all the world was waking to new life and she alone was going nowhere.

From her bedroom window she could see the sea, almost as far as the harbour and the *Santa Maria*, the boat on which she'd first known danger: not the danger of nearly drowning, but the first stirrings of desire and emotion for her fiancé's brother.

How terrible everything would have been if the wedding had gone ahead. Baptista had been right about that. For she no longer believed that making love with Lorenzo would have deadened her to Renato. It would have done the opposite. The more she'd discovered about physical passion, the more she would have craved the man who could make passion absolute for her. And that would not have been Lorenzo.

Instead she was married to the man she wanted, perhaps loved.

She sighed, realising that there was always a perhaps. She was holding back, refusing to admit to herself that she loved a man she wasn't sure was capable of love. Renato lived his life on very precise terms. What he wanted, he found a way to have. Just now he wanted her, and in bed he was as pleased with their bargain as she was herself. But that wasn't love. She'd told Baptista that he knew nothing about the heart. She still feared that was true. And while she believed it, she couldn't open her own heart to him.

There was a knock on her door. It was Sara the maid returning some ornaments she'd taken for washing. As she was laying them out the phone rang on the bedside table.

'Hello,' Heather said, snatching it up. 'Lorenzo?'

He sounded strange and troubled. 'Heather, are you alone?'

'No, just a moment.' She signalled to Sara to leave. 'All right, I'm alone now.'

'I need to talk to you—but Renato mustn't know.' His voice became urgent. 'Nobody must know.'

'Lorenzo, what is it?'

'I want you to come to London.'

'What?'

'I need you. Please, it's important. There are things I—please, Heather, *please*—'

The words poured out of him, frantic, desperate, and her refusal died on her lips.

'All right,' she said at last. 'I'll get the next plane. With luck I should be with you tonight.'

She found her passport and put a few things into an overnight bag, relieved that Baptista's absence gave her the chance to leave without answering questions.

She found Sara and said casually, 'I'll be back tomorrow, or maybe the next day.' Then she got out quickly. She couldn't tell the truth about where she was going or why.

Renato wasn't due home for a week, but the following afternoon he threw the house in turmoil by arriving early, striding into the house like a man with no time to waste. He was smiling, picturing his wife's face at seeing him early, and hearing that he'd abandoned a week's work to return to her. Perhaps she would even relax the slight distance he still felt she kept between them.

'*Amor mia,*' he called, throwing open the door to their bedroom. 'Where are you?'

The room was empty. He shrugged and went quickly downstairs. She would be on the terrace, probably talking with his mother. Or perhaps she was at the estate. Why had he gone first to their bedroom? He grinned, knowing full well why.

'Sara, where is my wife?'

The maid paused as she crossed the hall. She looked worried.

'I don't know, *signore*. Signor Lorenzo called yesterday, and after that she left in a great hurry.'

'Did she say where she was going?'

'No, *signore*. Only that she would be back today, or perhaps tomorrow.'

'Where is my mother?'

'Lying down in her room.'

He opened Baptista's door quietly, but she was sound asleep. He would have to bear his soul in patience. But the question went round and round in his head. What could Lorenzo have said to make Heather leave so quickly?

Renato went to his study and tried to settle to work. For an hour he managed more or less well. At least, he thought he was managing well. Then he put the phone down on a long conversation and realised that he couldn't remember a word of it. After that he gave up and called Lorenzo in London.

Lorenzo wasn't staying at the Ritz this time but at a newly opened luxury hotel that the firm was hoping to supply. As soon as the phone was answered Renato said, 'Lorenzo Martelli's room, please.'

'I'm sorry sir, but Mr Martelli checked out a few hours ago.'

Renato sat up straight. 'This morning? I understood he was there for a week.'

'So did we, sir. But after Mrs Martelli arrived yesterday they decided to leave early.'

'Mrs—Martelli? Do you mean the young English lady?'

'That's right. Mrs Heather Martelli. They checked out of their room this morning.'

The blow over the heart almost winded him. He didn't know how he managed to replace the phone. All the nerves seemed to have died in his hands, and his body was cold with shock.

He ought to have seen this coming. He'd always known that Lorenzo still lingered in her heart, but he'd charged ahead, arranging things as he wanted, as he always did, only to see them disintegrate in his hands.

Suddenly he couldn't breathe. It was like being caught in an avalanche with snow swirling around you from the back, the sides, the top—no way of stopping it—and then it froze solid about you.

He wanted to howl and fight his way out, but he was trapped, unable to move because he didn't know which move was the right one. He only knew that he wanted to turn time back to before this nightmare started. And he couldn't.

His wife had betrayed him with his brother. Thinking he would be away for another week, she'd hurried back to England to be with Lorenzo.

No, it was impossible. If it came out it would break Baptista's heart, and Heather would never do that to her. Renato tried to tell himself that she would never do it to *him*, but somehow the words wouldn't come.

It was impossible because of the kind of person she was, honest, decent, incapable of deceit. But only recently she'd said to him, 'What do you and I know of each other? In bed, everything. Outside, nothing.'

He was brought out of his reverie by the sound of a car drawing up outside. Moving like an automaton, he went out, and was in time to see the taxi door open and his brother emerge, looking dishevelled. Lorenzo, the dandy who would agonise over the perfect tie, was unshaven and his clothes looked rumpled.

He met Renato's eyes, made a helpless gesture, indicating that he couldn't face talking now, and went into the house.

'I need a shower,' he declared, and passed on up the stairs.

Renato made a gesture for Heather to join him in his study. As she walked past him he could hear his heart hammering. His whole life hung on the next few moments, what he would ask and what she would answer.

'What are you doing back so early?' she asked.

'Never mind that. Where in damnation have you been?'

Riled by his tone, she retorted crisply, 'I've been to London.'

'Without telling anyone where you were going, or why.'

'There were very good reasons for that.'

'I'll bet there were.'

Something in his voice made her look at him sharply. 'Be careful, Renato. I'm tired and I'm out of patience. If you've got something to say, say it.'

'Very well. Did you spend last night in his room?'

Heather stared at him in amazement. 'What—?'

'Answer me, damn you! Did you spend last night in Lorenzo's room?'

Her eyes flashed with temper. 'Yes,' she said. 'What are you accusing me of?'

'It's plain enough, isn't it? You always clung onto your image of him, no matter what he did. You're a fool, and I was a fool to marry you.'

'Well, nobody forced you to,' she cried. 'You were the one who insisted on this marriage.'

'Yes, and I'm well repaid for it. I thought you were the most wonderful woman in the world. I thought all beauty and honour lived in you—the one true and honest woman in a world of greedy deceivers. I knew you didn't love me when we married but we had time and I let myself believe—but the minute my back was turned you go to him—to his room, to his bed.'

'Renato—'

'Did you sleep in his bed?'

'Yes,' she yelled.

It was only now that he knew how desperately he'd longed to hear her deny it. It was undeniable, but surely she would find a way to make the terrible truth untrue. There was a roaring in his ears. It was like suffering the agonies of death, except that he stayed alive and died again and again.

Renato was a Sicilian. In this society a faithless wife could cause a blood feud that could last a century. But the only thought in his mind was to implore her to take back her words, let it be as it was before, let him believe in her again. Because if she was a deceiver then nothing in the world was worth anything.

'Do you know what you've just said?' he asked hoarsely. 'No, don't answer.' He held up an arm as if to ward her off. 'Perhaps it was time you said it. Or perhaps I should have listened long ago, when you tried to tell me there was no hope for me. But I'm not good at hearing what it doesn't suit me to hear, as you've often mentioned.'

'Renato—what are you saying?'

He gave a bark of mirthless laughter. 'I'm saying I give in. You've won—you and that boy who's wound himself around your heart so tightly that I can't find a way in. If you want him you can have him. I'll make it easy for you.'

'You mean—you'd free me to marry Lorenzo?'

'What else can I do?'

'What about Mamma?'

'She'll be all right if she sees that I'm perfectly happy about it.'

'And are you—perfectly happy?'

He didn't answer her in words but the truth was there in his eyes. He was dying inside.

'You survived something like this,' he said quietly. 'Maybe you can teach me how.'

'But—happy?'

'That isn't your concern any more. We could have been happy. Or at least I thought we could. I loved you, and I thought in time I could win your love. I hadn't reckoned on your heart being so stubborn and awkward. Why do you think I used my mother as an intermediary? Because I knew it was too soon for you to have got over him. If I'd approached you myself, talking of love, it would only have driven you off further.'

'But you knew—I mean there were things between us even then—'

'Yes, desire, not love. Sometimes I felt you wanted me, but with your body, not your heart. That wasn't mine, and if only you knew how much I wanted it, to have you look at me as I'd seen you look at him. I tried to keep it businesslike, not to alarm you, but that day in the temple—well—' He sighed. 'I couldn't always stick to my good intentions. And all the time I loved you so desperately that I thought you'd see and understand. But you never saw, because you never wanted to. It was all Lorenzo with you.

'We talked, once, about our day on the boat and what might have happened. You said you'd been in love with him, and I said love was a complication even when it was an illusion. If you knew how hard I prayed for you to say then that your love for him had been an illusion. I was holding my breath, willing you to say it—but you didn't. And I suppose I knew the truth.'

His face was as bleak as a winter's day, and for the first time his eyes weren't closed to her, but open, defenceless, letting her see the suffering man within. She put her hand out but he flinched away from it. She couldn't speak. Everything in her was concentrated on hearing what he would say next.

'I should have let you go then,' he said at last, 'and this wouldn't have needed to happen. Well, it's happened. I brought it on myself, and I make no complaint.'

'I don't believe it's you I'm hearing say all this,' she breathed.

'No? Well, I've been unlike myself since I knew you.' He took a shuddering breath. 'I'll make it easy for you, but go quickly. I'm not sure how long I can keep this up.'

'Renato—'

'For God's sake go!' His face was livid. 'Get out of here, and *never let me see you again.*'

CHAPTER TWELVE

SHE took a step towards him. 'I'm not going anywhere. You're my husband and I love you, and I'm staying right here with you.'

'Don't play games with me,' he said hoarsely. 'You've already told me that you slept with him.'

'I said no such thing. I've said that I slept in Lorenzo's bed last night—' in her eagerness she seized his arms and gave him a little shake '—but I didn't say that Lorenzo was there with me.'

'What?' he whispered.

His wretchedness made her heart ache. 'Oh, darling!' She touched his face. 'What a fool you are! While I was sleeping in Lorenzo's bed, *he* was sleeping in a police cell.'

'What—did—you—say?'

'He wasn't with me. He spent the night *under lock and key*, sleeping on a bunk, with a blanket. Why do you think he looks as if he's slept in his clothes? Because he has.'

He stared at her as her words pierced his cloud of misery. And suddenly the sun shone more brilliantly, the steeple bells rang and the trumpets sounded a fanfare.

'A police cell?' he echoed, as though repeating her words was all he could do.

'He called me yesterday from a police station in London. He'd been arrested for driving under the influence and taking a swipe at a policeman. I figured I'd better get over there fast. Mamma was out and I thought the

175

fewer people who knew about it the better, so I just caught the first plane to London.

'I arrived yesterday evening and went straight to the station, but I couldn't get him out because they were afraid he'd skip the country. So he had to spend the night in the cell. I stayed in his hotel room. It seemed silly to pay for another when his was empt—'

She was silenced by the crushing pressure of his mouth on hers. There were no words for the feelings that possessed them. For each the declaration of love had come in the unlikeliest way, catching them unawares, trapping them into admissions that their pride might have made impossible for years. Joy, triumph and blazing, overwhelming relief mingled in their kiss, lighting up the world.

'Tell me it's true,' he said against her mouth. 'Promise me that I won't wake up in a minute—kiss me—kiss me—'

'It's all true, I swear it. I never slept with Lorenzo.'

'No, not that—the other thing you said—about loving me—'

'I do love you, Renato. There's nobody I want but you. But I never thought you'd say you love me.'

'Does a man go insane for a woman, the way I have, unless he loves her?'

'You always had so many good reasons that were nothing to do with love.'

'Fool's reasons. I swore I'd never let a woman matter that much to me again. And then I met you, but it was already too late because you loved another man. I had to tell myself anything except that I loved you.' He kissed her fiercely again and again. 'I've been so afraid...'

Lost in happiness, she was only vaguely aware that she was moving, climbing, somehow they were upstairs. The sudden sound was the door of their bedroom being kicked shut then their clothes being hastily torn off as they reached feverishly for each other.

They made love like people who'd met for the first time. There was pleasure, but also relief and reassurance. Above all there was boundless hope. Only a few minutes ago the future hadn't existed. Now it stretched to infinity, full of joy and fulfilment.

'I suppose we ought to get up,' Heather said at last, reluctantly. 'Mamma will be awake, and she'll wonder why Lorenzo is home. I wonder what he's telling her. We must find out and make sure we don't give him away.'

'You wrong Lorenzo,' Renato said at once. 'He'll tell her the truth. Whatever else you can say about him—and you can say a good deal—he's honest.'

'Yes. Do you realise how much we owe his honesty?'

But Renato didn't answer, and she realised that his wounds were still raw, and he had some way to go yet.

'Tell me the rest of the story,' he said at last. 'What happened? Did you spring him from gaol? Are the two of you on the run?'

'Luckily, desperate measures weren't needed. I got him a lawyer, and first thing this morning he was up before the magistrate. It wasn't very serious. He was only a little bit over the limit, and there was no accident, nobody hurt.'

'What about assaulting the policeman?'

'It was just a little swipe. He barely touched him. He was fined and bound over to keep the peace. I know he has a lot of appointments in England but I thought I'd better get him back here quickly.'

'You did the right thing. I won't send him back for a while. But somebody has to visit his customers, and you're the best person. You did brilliantly on that Scottish trip—'

'Brilliantly? You were breathing down my neck—checking up on me—'

He kissed her. 'It's nice to know I'm not the only fool in the family. I went to Scotland because I couldn't stand being apart from you another day.'

She snuggled against him, wondering if Lorenzo's proximity in England might also have had something to do with it. But she didn't ask. She no longer needed to.

'So there it is,' he murmured, 'the last piece in that jigsaw you were talking about. We fit it exactly.'

'It's odd, I'm not quite sure—' She brooded.

'If we love each other, what else can there be?'

'I don't know. It's just that I have an odd feeling that there are still two pieces missing.'

'Forget it,' he said, holding her tightly. 'We've found each other. I'd nearly given up hope of that happening.'

She let it go and snuggled against him, revelling in her happiness. But the thought wouldn't be entirely dismissed that the jigsaw wasn't quite complete.

Two pieces to go.

She made the trip to England and returned to be plunged into the preparations for Baptista's birthday party, to be given in the Great Hall of the Residenza.

'We can kill two birds with one stone,' Renato said to her one evening. 'You know I've been thinking of branching out into flowers. There are some that we grow here better than anywhere else in the world, and it's an area you might take charge of.'

'I'd love to,' she said eagerly.

'Then you should start meeting some of the specialist growers. 'I'm especially interested in this man,' he said, handing her a business card bearing the name Vincenzo Tordone. 'He has acres of greenhouses that can supply

everything in winter. I'd like you to look him over and
let me know what you think. If his stuff is high quality
we can use him to fill the house with flowers on Mamma's
birthday, and set up a deal afterwards.'

Pleased, Heather visited Vincenzo Tordone in his office
in Palermo. He was a tall, thin man in his late sixties,
with white hair and a gently courteous manner that won
her over at once. He took her on a visit to his glass-
covered acres just outside the city, and she marvelled at
the variety of perfect blooms that flourished under his
hands.

'I have a business in Rome,' he told her as they sipped
Marsala afterwards. 'It's a good business. My wife was
Roman, and when she was alive she helped me to run it.
Now she's dead I've handed the reins to my son and
daughter, and returned to my home.'

'You're Sicilian, then?'

'Oh, yes. I was born in this country, and lived here
until my twenties. One day I shall die and be buried here.'
He sighed with pleasure. 'This is the best land in the
world to grow plants. There's nowhere so fertile, nowhere
else where the flowers raise their heads so eagerly.'

He made her talk about herself, and she gave a carefully
edited description of how she had come from England and
ended up marrying into the Martelli family.

'Do you find our ways strange?' he asked courteously.

'Not really. Everyone has been so kind, especially my
mother-in-law, Baptista. She took me under her wing right
from the start. She even gave me her own estate of Bella
Rosaria.'

'Ah, yes, I've heard of it—who has not? They say the
flowers there are very fine.'

'They are, especially the rose bushes. Some of them

have been there for years. She tends and protects them like children.'

They plunged into a discussion of the best way to make rose bushes long-lasting. She liked the simple old man, and when she got home it was a pleasure to be able to tell Renato honestly that his blooms were first-rate. The deal was duly signed, covering the export of his produce both from Sicily and Rome, with a separate deal covering the provision of flowers for the party.

On the day Baptista spent the afternoon asleep, so as to be at her best for the evening. She rose bright-eyed and cheerful and sat calmly while her maid arrayed her in pearls. When Renato and Heather looked in, she took his hand and said in a pleading voice, 'My son, this may be my last birthday on earth—'

'Mamma, you say that every year,' he reminded her tenderly.

'And it's true every year. But this year there is one special gift that I long for above all others.'

'It's yours if it's in my power.'

'If I could believe that there is truly no more bad blood between you and your brother—'

'Believe it. That was over long ago.'

Baptista smiled, but Heather sensed that she had hoped for something more.

There was a knock on the door, and Bernardo and Lorenzo entered, one carrying wine, the other glasses, to toast their mother privately before the festivities began.

When they had all saluted her Baptista half rose to go, but Renato said, 'Stay a moment. I have another toast.' When he was sure he had everyone's attention he said, 'I drink to my brother, Lorenzo, to whose courage and honesty I owe my happiness. I made a terrible mistake that almost destroyed three lives. When we went to the cathe-

dral, all three of us knew that that marriage ought never
to take place. But it seemed too late. The juggernaut was
grinding on and nobody knew how to stop it. Only one
person found the nerve to halt it in its tracks. My brother,
you gave me the woman I love, and for this I thank you
with all my heart.'

'And so do I,' Heather said happily.

Baptista was weeping with joy. Lorenzo looked about
to sink with embarrassment. Renato set down his glass
and seized him in a bear hug while Bernardo thumped
them both on the back.

'Thank you,' Heather whispered when Renato had returned to her.

'I should have said it long ago.'

One piece down and one to go.

It was time for the party to begin. As Baptista descended
on Renato's arm, to applause from the assembled guests,
the profusion of blooms made her stop and gasp with
pleasure.

'They are so beautiful, my dears,' she said as she settled
in the throne-like chair from which she would preside over
the evening. 'Thank you.'

'There is one more thing,' Renato said. 'The man who
arranged all this would like to offer you his own congratulations, with a special gift.'

'That is very kind of him.'

'But—' Renato looked a little uncertain. 'Mamma, are
you strong enough for a little shock—if it is a happy one?'

'Certainly. You have prepared me. Is Signor Tordone
going to give me a shock?'

'I think he just might.'

Renato nodded and a servant opened the door. Through

it came the tall figure of Vincenzo. He walked calmly towards Baptista, never taking his eyes from her.

Nor did she take her eyes from him. As Heather watched she half rose from her seat, then fell back with a little gasp. Her hand flew to her throat as Vincenzo came to stand before her, holding in his hand one perfect red rose.

Baptista didn't seem to see it. All her attention was for the old man's face, and at last a glad cry broke from her.

'Fede!' she said in joyful disbelief. *'Fede!'*

'I don't believe it!' Heather gasped. 'That can't be—'

'It is,' Renato grinned. 'His real name is Federico Marcello. My grandfather was a fearsome character, but never quite the monster people thought. He drove Federico out of Sicily with threats and ordered him to change his name so that Mamma couldn't trace him. But then he arranged for friends to help him get started in his own business, and put quite a lot of work his way.'

'But how did you find him?'

'I set a private enquiry agent onto it. He traced him to Rome and then all the way back here. I was fairly sure who he was when you went to see him, but when you told me about the talk you had, that clinched it.'

'But why didn't you tell me?'

Renato gave her a strange look. 'Perhaps I wanted to surprise you, too. I wonder if I have.'

'Yes,' she said slowly. 'I thought I knew you, but I never imagined that you could think of this.'

He touched her cheek gently. 'It takes a lifetime to know someone, my dearest.'

'And we have a lifetime,' she whispered.

'Do we?'

'Yes. I wasn't sure. But I am now.'

Her heart rejoiced at what she had discovered tonight.

Renato was a proud, difficult man, who would never be easy to live with. But he understood things about love that even she had never dreamed of. This hadn't been only to please his mother. It had also been to prove something to herself that he couldn't have explained in words.

Something caught in her throat as she saw Baptista and Fede sitting side by side, their hands entwined. Moving very quietly, she and Renato crept close enough to hear.

'I returned to Sicily to be close to you,' Fede was saying. 'But I never dared to hope that you would recognise me.'

'I knew you at once,' Baptista said through her joyful tears.

'And I would have known you anywhere. You are just as you have lived in my heart, all these years.'

'All these years.' She said the words slowly. 'And yet I hope you haven't been alone. I would rather think of you having a good life, even without me.'

'Then think it,' Fede said firmly. 'My wife was a wonderful woman. She gave me two fine children, and while she lived we were devoted.' His voice changed. 'But it was not with her as it had been with you.'

'Yes,' Baptista murmured. 'Yes, that's just how it was.'

He kissed her hand. 'We have done our duty to others. Now we may think of ourselves for the time that is left.'

The last guest had gone. The house was quiet as Renato and Heather, arms entwined, climbed the stairs in the semi-darkness.

'They really mean it,' Heather said in wonder. 'When they look at each other they see what used to be.'

'Or maybe they see what truly is,' Renato suggested. 'They see a truth that years and wrinkles can never change.'

'Will it be like that with us?'

'I can only speak for myself. And I tell you that no other woman will ever hold my heart. If you were to die tomorrow I would live alone for the rest of my life, rather than try to replace you. I think Mamma and Fede were each right to marry other people. That's the sensible way. But I can't be sensible where you're concerned. Without you, my life would be only a long wait until we could be together again.'

'And I—'

'Hush!' He laid a gentle hand over her lips. 'Don't say it unless it's true.'

'Do you think my love is less than yours?'

'I don't ask. It doesn't matter. As long as you love me a little. Where you are concerned, I have never been as proud as I seemed. I can live on crumbs.'

It was true. His pride was gone, replaced by a trust in his beloved that made pride needless. She saw it in his eyes, heard it in the gentleness of his voice.

'Not crumbs,' she whispered. 'But a feast.' She took his hand, led him to their room and opened the door. 'Come,' she said as she drew him inside. 'Let me tell you about it.'

The last piece in place.

Lying quietly in her bed that night, Baptista listened until she heard the sound of two sets of footsteps climbing the stairs and going along the corridor. They moved slowly, as if the owners were drifting contentedly, their arms about each other. Outside Heather and Renato's room they stopped. Baptista's sharp ears caught the soft murmur of voices, then the click as the door opened, and another one as it closed.

She smiled to herself in the darkness. She had been

right all along. When her time came, she could go in peace, knowing that her son had found deep, lasting love.

But perhaps her time wouldn't come so soon after all. She had much to live for, including the child that Heather was carrying. Not that Heather knew yet, but she, Baptista knew. A grandson would be nice, but perhaps a little girl would be better. A girl, to wind herself around her father's heart and teach him about love.

And yet, already he'd shown that he knew more about true love than either his mother or his wife had guessed. Who would have imagined that it would be Renato who brought Fede back to her, that he would have understood…?

However much time she had left, Fede would be there. He had promised to visit her every day, and they would sit together talking, or just holding hands. Like hers his body was aged and his face wrinkled, but she had looked into his eyes and known that he was still Fede.

This she owed to Renato, who'd been rescued from harshness and cynicism by the one woman who'd known how to reach him.

And then there was Bernardo, her son and yet not her son, a man with a wild, dark heart that allowed nobody inside. She thought of Angie, the young English woman who had loved him but been defeated by his pride. At least, men called it pride. Baptista called it stupidity. Angie might have saved him. In fact, she still might if certain plans of Baptista's worked out as she meant them to.

A knowing gleam came into her eye. Death could wait until she was ready. There were things to do. Arrangements to make. Heads to knock together. She was feeling stronger every moment….

PARENTS WANTED

Families in the making!

In the orphanage of a small Australian town
called Bay Beach are little children desperately
in need of love, and dreaming of their very
own family....

The answer to their dreams can also be found
in Bay Beach! Couples who are destined for
each other—even if they don't know it yet.
Brought together by love for these tiny
children, can they find true love themselves—
and finally become a real family?

Titles in this series by fan-favorite
MARION LENNOX are

A Child in Need—(April HR #3650)
Their Baby Bargain—(July HR #3662)

Look out for further Parents Wanted stories
in Harlequin Romance®, coming soon!

Available wherever Harlequin Books are sold.

HARLEQUIN®
Makes any time special ®

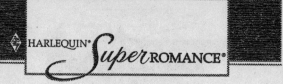

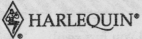